The Tiger's Daughter

The Tiger's Daughter

❧ Bharati Mukherjee

HOUGHTON MIFFLIN COMPANY *BOSTON 1972*

THIRD PRINTING W

Library of Congress Catalog Card Number: 77–162011
ISBN: 0–395–12715–7

Printed in the United States of America

For my mother and father
and my husband, Clark

Part One

1

THE CATELLI-CONTINENTAL HOTEL on Chowringhee Avenue, Calcutta, is the navel of the universe. Gray and imposing, with many bay windows and fake turrets, the hotel occupies half a block, then spills untidily into an intersection. There are no spacious grounds or circular driveways, only a small square courtyard and a dry fountain. The entrance is small, almost shabby, marked by a sun-bleached awning and two potted hibiscus shrubs. The walls and woodwork are patterned with mold and rust around vertical drains. The sidewalks along the hotel front are painted with obscenities and political slogans that have been partially erased.

A first-floor balcony where Europeans drank tea in earlier decades cuts off the sunlight from the sidewalk. In the daytime this is a gloomy place; only a colony of beggars take advantage of the shade, to roll out their torn mats or rearrange their portable ovens and cardboard boxes. The area directly in front of the Catelli's doorway is littered with vendors' trays, British mystery novels and old magazines laid out on burlap sacks, and fly-blackened banana slices sold by shriveled women. At night neon tubes from tiny storefronts flicker over sleeping bodies outside the hotel, then die before the breaking of the violent Calcutta dawn.

The Catelli is guarded by a turbaned young man, who sits on a stool all day and stares at three paintings by local expressionists on permanent display by the hibiscus shrubs. He is unusual for a doorman of any hotel; he is given to sullen quietness rather than simple arrogance, as though he detects horror in the lives of the anonymous businessmen who pass through his doors each day. A doorman is an angel, he seems to say. He is not without love, however, this guardian of the Catelli-Continental Hotel. He loves the few guests who come every day but do not stay. He sees flurries of exquisite young women in pale cottons and silks and elegant old men carrying puppies and canes, and he worships them. While small riots break out in the city, while buses burn and workers surround the warehouses, these few come to the Catelli for their daily ritual of espresso or tea. And the doorman gathers them in with an emotional salute.

There is, of course, no escape from Calcutta. Even an angel concedes that when pressed. Family after family moves from the provinces to its brutish center, and the center quivers a little, absorbs the bodies, digests them, and waits.

2

IN THE YEAR 1879 by the English calendar, on a Monday in Sravan, the month of heaviest rains, Hari Lal Banerjee of Pachapara was standing under a wedding canopy on the roof of his house, once a happy rajah's palace.

Hari Lal stood by the parapet, head unprotected by the red and yellow canopy, legs slightly apart under a fine white *dhoti*, as he watched tenants and workers gather in the covered courtyard below to celebrate the wedding of his children. It was a lonely watch, and his mind kept straying beyond the compound walls to the night beaten by rains.

On other nights Hari Lal might have ridden into that darkness. He knew the territory well, the greenish-black soil, the sudden creeks and canals and treacherous rivers. He claimed no virtue in retreat, he had no desire to exaggerate the safety of ancestral houses. But on this auspicious Monday, chilled and shuddering in spite of astrologers' assurances, he was glad to return to the shelter of canvas awnings on bamboo stakes. The rain fell steadily in his compound. Small drops trickled down the red and yellow tassels of canopies and dampened the heads of little boys and servants. Some children, wearing leaf hats, floated paper boats in open drains. The barber's son, almost a grown man, dashed out of the canvas shelter and danced clumsily to amuse his friends. They did not hear the straining and imprisoned ghost of change.

Hari Lal's friends, men in their thirties carrying gold-headed canes, detected nothing unusual either. They had patterned their lives around kerosene lamps; now the hissing strings of wedding lights on the roof gave them a sense of mastery over the wet blackness.

"It's a happy night," they said. "It's an auspicious night." They did not expect their lives to be spoiled by astrological errors or fatal paradoxes. A loud sentimentality preyed on these guests. They talked about the stability of Hindu marriages, they came back again and again to the bounty of the Bengali soil and to the orderliness of their little villages. They told their servants to bring out more lights, the *shanai*-players to play with more feeling, and their wives to serve them more vegetable chops and shrimp cutlets. They twirled their gold-headed canes and gossiped and behaved like perfect wedding guests.

But the host stood his lonely watch on the roof, listening to the anguished music of the *shanai*-players. There were no lessons or insights for Hari Lal that night, only a premonition of small violences. He saw little cracks and holes appear in the soil that he thought he knew well, and the rain poured steadily, expanding the openings rather than filling them. His first impulse was to protect his friends, though he knew the night beyond the canopies was more savage, more permanent than the enemies fought by other Banerjee men from Pachapara.

While Hari Lal stood ready, and the musicians played fiercely, the guests from the courtyard were brought to the roof for the wedding feast. Young men busied themselves with brass pails of rice, ran up and down staircases with pitchers of drinking water. Hari Lal's nephews walked between rows of diners, slopping out *pilau* and saffron rice, fried eggplant and pumpkin, potatoes, peas, curried fish and curried mutton, lemon wedges, yoghurt, tamarind, seven kinds of chutneys and ten kinds of sweetmeats. They deposited all this extravagantly on banana leaves to be eaten, digested or carried away by two thousand relatives and guests. The village beggars, no longer ill at ease in the bejeweled gathering, sat in their assigned rows and joked with vegetarian Brahmin apprentices. They watched the elegant Banerjee nephews in silk shirts and gold buttons, and they yielded to the small, secret appeals of aristocratic dress.

In the exact center of the roof burned a sacrificial fire. The wedding ceremonies had suddenly quickened their pace. The moment of indissoluble ties was at hand. The crowd tensed. Virgins dreamed of fulfillment; married women of joys that had been promised them. Hari Lal moved toward the fire to take his part in the wedding rites. He moved past lines of beautiful golden women, past mango leaves in copper pots, a baggy-eyed priest and his earnest assistant, two young men in nuptial crowns, till he reached his weeping little girls in adult bridal ornaments.

Did Hari Lal, his arms around his daughters, guess then the shape and intentions of the dark night? As he grasped the final stunted issue of the Pachapara Banerjees perhaps he only foresaw his own death. The shadows of suicide or exile, of Bengali soil sectioned and ceded, of workers rising against their bosses could not have been divined by even a wise man in those days.

3

CHANGES IN THE ANATOMIES of nations or continents are easy to perceive. But changes wrought by gods or titans are too subtle for measurement. At first the human mind suffers premonitions, then it learns to submit.

Life in Pachapara continued to be pleasant enough. There were many more marriages, and of course many deaths. The death of Hari Lal Banerjee was loudly mourned by villagers. He had been a good man, a strong man; he had never protested his fate. Two summers after his daughters' wedding he had ridden out of his compound to stop a feud, and someone with a knife had leaped on him from flowering bushes.

With Hari Lal's death the Banerjee family lost its hold on Pachapara. The Banerjees were replaced by the Jute Mill Roy Chowdhurys, and they too produced good and virile men. But the Roy Chowdhurys thought it prudent to lock the gates of their estate and to replace each brick pried loose by violence. Outside their compound, sometimes on the bathing-steps of rivers, or in red dirt alleys that led to the marketplace, they saw angry, fanatical faces. There were more unreasonable murders, suspicious drownings, bloody and mutilated bodies discovered in paddy fields. There were also more communal riots. Eventually Pachapara was apportioned on the map as foreign soil and Hari Lal's marble study became the parlor of a Moslem butcher. By then it was too late for the villagers to remark on the anatomy of change.

But long before that, Santana, Hari Lal's eldest daughter, left Pachapara with her husband. Santana's husband, a barrister, was not a man of vision; prospects of change excited him. After Hari Lal's sudden death, he sold the moldy Banerjee house he had inherited by marriage and moved to Calcutta. The village, he thought, would only exhaust his strength. Certainly the big city developed talents and emotions that the barrister hardly suspected in himself.

Though Santana's husband was successful in Calcutta he remained humble, at least on the surface. He made his points in court so decently that he was often invited to British clubs by liberal young Englishmen, though never of course to the Calcutta Sunbathing Association, where flabby Englishwomen surrendered their charms to the gratified stares of *pukka* Englishmen.

The barrister's success led to one fateful act. In a year of colonial unrest, in spite of warnings from friendly British colleagues and anxious Bengali gentlemen, he defended two teenage Brahmin nationalists. This action was unfortunately construed not as the necessity of conscience but as deliberate imprudence, and the barrister was unofficially reprimanded.

In aristocratic anger Santana's husband withdrew from the Bar, bought a lumberyard in Assam and a tobacco factory in Calcutta and insulated himself still further from the British, the insults, the dread.

Arupa, Hari Lal's younger daughter, who had from infancy shown signs of chronic nervousness, was abandoned by her husband in the first weeks of marriage. In time the young woman lost her beauty and her strength. In time she became a legend in Pachapara, an eerie shape beneath the red cotton quilt of her bridal four-poster, her hair cropped close as a gesture of defiance, her limbs bare of all ornaments, her eyes cold and accusing. Occasionally driven by some memory or anger, she would steal from under her quilt, unlock from a drawer her bridal photograph yellowing in its silver frame, and stare at the man who was still her husband.

*

So slight were the initial changes among the families of Bengali *zamindars*. An imprisoned and gigantic spirit had begun to move, and all things on its body — towns, buildings, men — were slowly altering their shapes. The alterations were not yet impressive; none suspected they might be fatal. Years later a young woman who had never been to Pachapara would grieve for the Banerjee family and try to analyze the reasons for its change. She would sit by a window in America to dream of Hari Lal, her great-grandfather, and she would wonder at the gulf that separated him from herself. But her dreams and her straining would yield a knowledge that was visionless.

4

NOW IN THESE TIMES of disorder Calcutta had to admit that Bengal Tiger Banerjee was not like other men. A strong man is a mediator between divine and mortal fates. While the restive city forced weak men to fanatical defiance or dishonesty, the Bengal Tiger remained powerful, just and fearless.

Calcutta was losing its memories in a bonfire of effigies, buses and trams. But the Bengal Tiger continued to inoculate himself against the city, improving and expanding the tobacco firm he had received as his dowry, working out medical and disability insurances for his workers, night classes in the factory for those who could not write or read. Outside his house on Camac Street and his Barrackpore factory, men were responding with threats or heroism to the sullenness of Calcutta; but the Bengal Tiger remained jovial and impartial, absorbed in his duties, his business, and his charities.

Beneath that stern affability, however, there must have run a deep suspicion or pain, which had urged the Bengal Tiger to send his only child, a girl of fifteen, out of India for college.

The motives for that decision remained his secret, but its consequences were terrifying. It had put a rather fragile young woman on a jet for Poughkeepsie, and left out of account the limits of her courage and common sense.

For Tara Vassar had been an almost unsalvageable mistake. If she had not been a Banerjee, a Bengali Brahmin, the great-granddaughter of Hari Lal Banerjee, or perhaps if she had not been trained by the good nuns at St. Blaise's to remain composed and ladylike in all emergencies, she would have rushed home to India at the end of her first week.

"Dearest Mummy and Daddy," she began a hundred times. But there was no way she could confide to her parents the exquisite new pains, no way she dared explain that in Poughkeepsie her love of Johnny Mathis was deep and sincere. As each atom of newness bombarded her she longed for Camac Street, where she had grown up. Tara's Camac Street friends did not forget her. They wrote her long and beautiful letters, meticulously addressed with periods and commas. In their letters they complained wittily of boredom in Calcutta, the movies at the Metro, the foul temper of the whiskered nun from Mauritius, the weather's beastliness, but not once did they detect Tara's fears. These friends who had never left home envied her freedom; they asked for records and transparent nighties; they were ecstatic when she told them she had seen Johnny Mathis in person.

Tara saw herself being pushed to the periphery of her old world, and to save herself she clung to the loyalties of the Camac Street girls. For them she stood in line at the post office, hugging poorly wrapped parcels of shampoos and lipsticks, trying to understand the jokes of the ill-tempered Negro clerk.

The girls in the residence hall tried to draw her out. They

lent her books and records and hand lotions unasked. But how could Tara share her Camac Street thoughts with the pale, dry-skinned girls the same way they shared their Alberto VO[5] in the shower? At first she was polite, and anxious to make her contribution.

"My great-grandfather's name was Hari Lal Banerjee. He was a very plucky man." But such remarks she found made a bad impression and soon she gave up.

Little things pained her. If her roommate did not share her bottle of mango chutney she sensed discrimination. Three weeks in Poughkeepsie and I am undone, thought Tara. Three weeks and I must defend my family, my country, my Johnny Mathis. No previous test, not the overseas Cambridge School Leaving Certificate Examination, not even the labor unrest at her father's factory had prepared her for this. She prayed to Kali for strength so she would not break down before these polite Americans. And Kali, who was a mother nursing her infant, serene, black, exquisite, and Kali, who was a mother devouring her infant, furious, black and exquisite, who sat under silk saris in a suitcase at Vassar, smiled out at her mischievously.

Later Tara was fond of saying that she had first started to think for herself in the dormitory at Vassar. That may not be quite accurate. But she did stay up till two in the morning discussing birth control with her dormitory neighbors. At St. Blaise's she had not been permitted to think about sex; love was all right if it could be linked to the poetry of Francis Thompson or Alice Meynell. But now, realizing the girls identified her with the population explosion, the loop, vasectomy in railway stations, she blossomed into a bedside intellectual.

The topic of urban development was quite another matter. Tara had never been farther than Shambazar. She could not fully visualize tenements and beggars. Nor did she wish to talk about it. Dark skinny buildings, devious alleys, rotting garbage, idle men leaning against barred windows, child-beggars in front of food stalls: all this made her physically sick. She was a sensitive person, sensitive especially to places. She remembered in Calcutta the chauffeur had always carried smelling salts for her in the glove compartment. Her memory, elastic, warm and gentle, showed her families asleep on sidewalks, children curled in wooden crates, and this undermined her remarks.

In December of her first year abroad at a gathering of the Indian Students' Association in New York, Tara met a young man from Calcutta. His name was Manik (Mota) Mukherjee and he was studying political science at Columbia. Tara's imagination, in the custody of St. Blaise's nuns since the age of three, while not willingly touching on sex, quite often centered on love. She fancied herself in love with Mota. Though she did not confide in anyone, not even in the Camac Street girls who had seemed ghostly by December, her father was quick to detect her concealed emotion.

> I met one Mr. Chakravorty [wrote the Bengal Tiger] at yesterday's meeting of chamber of commerce. He is brother-in-law of one Mr. Mukherjee who has one son, Manik (Mota), who has been aforementioned. We had whiskey together (prices have gone up), and frank chat. He told me this boy is very, very brilliant, and everyone loves him . . .

When Tara read this letter from her father she could no longer concentrate on her term papers. The Bengal Tiger knew that she had fallen in love, but he had not lost his temper. Three days later she received another urgent letter.

> We have had further talks with the same Mr. Chakravorty, brother-in-law of same Mr. Mukherjee. We have also made thorough independent inquiries at our end. His family is very much like ours, honest and happy-go-lucky. Remember love is nine-

tenths prudence, one-tenth physical attraction. Don't do anything foolish or rash. It is your happiness that I demand. Caste, class and province are more valuable in marriage than giddiness. We do not disapprove of this young man, but we're not there to guide you, Taramoni. It may be only fair to indicate to the young chap that we are modernized people, and do not believe in dowry system. We will give from the bottom of our hearts as you well know, but do not on any account tell him that . . .

This advice brought tears to Tara's eyes. Her father was treating her as an adult. He who had been embarrassed when Rajah the cocker spaniel had mated was now frankly discussing dating and marriage with her. But the advice was never put to practical application. Before Tara could pursue her fancies about being in love, Manik (Mota) Mukherjee went to Sweden for a vacation, and on his return did not once call her.

Toward the end of May that first year abroad, as the girls around her prepared to go home, Tara was seized by a vision of terror. She saw herself sleeping in a large carton on a sidewalk while hatted men made impious remarks to her. Headless monsters winked at her from eyes embedded in pudgy shoulders. The sounds of classrooms and dorms were cut off by the cardboard sides of her carton. Not a strain of weather reports from someone's radio, no one scoring an emphatic point in a seminar, not even the smell of instant coffee in the corridor. She suffered fainting spells, headaches and nightmares. Her face took on the pinched and almost beautiful look of tragic heroines in Bengali dramas. She complained of homesickness in letters to her mother, who promptly prayed to Kali to save Tara's conscience, chastity and complexion.

The terror seethed in a lonely room at Vassar. It rushed out of borrowed drapes and pictures; it bounced off desktops and lumpy armchairs. Tara's academic adviser, who did not believe in emotion, watched with distaste the sudden defoliation of

Tara, and made it her business to keep the young woman occupied all summer.

"Let's see now," began the adviser. She had called Tara to her office, which was close, book-lined and rectangular. "Do you type?"

Tara thought a table lamp could throw cruel shadows on the face of a middle-aged spinster. "No," she answered, tracing the blotches of light and dark with an imaginary finger. "My father's secretary goes out of his way to help us. When Rajah, our cocker spaniel, died and we were so heartbroken, he even arranged a secret night burial for him without waiting for our permission. He's always done everything, all our typing et cetera. That's why I've never had to learn, you see."

The adviser, used to revealing herself only as a liberal missionary, failed to understand the import of Tara's remarks.

"I think you better go to summer school," she said with authority before a new complication could arise.

And so, after two semesters of reading primly in the library, of cycling blithely from class to class, of rubbing Nivea cream on her face to protect it from the hostile weather, Tara left obediently for summer school in Madison. Within fifteen minutes of her arrival at the Greyhound bus station there, in her anxiety to find a cab, she almost knocked down a young man. She did not know then that she eventually would marry that young man. But at that moment she merely said "Excuse me," and continued to drag her offensive luggage toward the taxi stand.

Part Two ❧

1

TARA's BOMBAY RELATIVES were all at the airport to welcome her. They had brought garlands and sweetmeats to put her at ease, but after the long flight, the awkward stops in transit lounges, and the clearing of customs she was groggy and nervous about meeting them. Little nephews whose names she did not catch were told to touch her feet in *pronam* when she was introduced to them as "the America auntie." The Bombay relatives hugged her and spoke to her in Bengali, the first she had heard since a Durga Pujah gathering in New York.

"Our poor Tultul!" they screamed at her. "How thin you have become!"

"And so much darker!"

"Tultul, we thought America would —"

She had not remembered the Bombay relatives' nickname for her. No one had called her Tultul in years; her parents called her Taramoni when they wanted to show special affection. It was difficult to listen to these strangers.

"My goodness, Tultul, I cannot tell you how bony you have become!"

"Where is your husband? How dare he not come!"

"We wanted to show off the American *jamai.*"

"Then the *Indian Ladies Weekly* would have taken our pictures!"

While the Bombay relatives exaggerated their disappointment that David had not accompanied her, Tara suspected they were relieved that he had not. The relatives lived in a large city but did not know many foreigners; David would have taxed their English too much.

"I'm very tired," said Tara. "Are we ready to go?"

"We are ready, we are ready. Where is the car?"

"You must promise not to look at the bad parts of India."

"Promise to keep your eyes shut! Some parts are horrible."

"What about the smell? She ought to cover her nose."

They drove her from the airport to their apartment on Marine Drive, which seemed to Tara run-down and crowded. Seven years earlier on her way to Vassar, she had admired the houses on Marine Drive, had thought them fashionable, but now their shabbiness appalled her. The relatives must have sensed her disappointment.

"Bombay flats are impossible. We pay nine hundred rupees!"

"To say nothing of the bribes and *pugris* to landlords!"

All the Bombay relatives begged her to spend at least a week on Marine Drive before going on to Calcutta. They agreed it was a shame that her father (whom they called the Bengal Tiger) had been held up at home by an unexpected general strike. Otherwise, they indicated, her reception at the airport would have been ten times more spectacular.

"What a tragedy Bengal Tiger couldn't be here! But what can he do with hooligans bothering Calcutta?"

"He always stays with us when he's here. Why do you fuss so much?"

"Such a hearty man our Bengal Tiger that even neighbors love to hear him laugh in the flat!"

They showed her the train tickets they had already bought for her and her father. But now that Tara had to travel alone to Calcutta the Bombay uncle was hesitant to hand over the tickets. A two-day journey in a compartment full of strangers he considered a dangerous experience for any Banerjee girl. He advised her to fly instead. On the joints of his fingers he enumerated his "very fine connections with the airplane people," and promised to get her plane reservations within the hour.

"Thank goodness things haven't degenerated Bombay-side so

far. I myself will fly with you. Two days' leave of absence from office. What is that?"

"She's our responsibility till she gets to Calcutta. Please let Uncle decide what is the best solution here."

But Tara would make no concession to their kindness. She was anxious to rest by herself, she explained; the train journey would be perfect as long as her compartment was air-conditioned. Though she saw the Bombay relatives pale at her stubbornness, she insisted she preferred to be alone so she could prepare for her vacation in Calcutta.

"Vacation!" cried the Bombay aunt. "How can I tell you how terrible Calcutta has become? *Arré baba!*"

"What nonsense you speak!" objected the uncle. "The papers Bombay-side are full of lies. Bombay is always jealous of Calcutta."

"But how will I explain to the Bengal Tiger we're sending you alone?" asked the Bombay aunt. "How dare you try to cause a misunderstanding, Tultul?"

Defeated and embarrassed, the relatives attributed Tara's improprieties to her seven years in America.

The next evening all the Bombay relatives and their servants came to the railway station to see her off. The uncle rushed ahead, keeping track of the coolie who had Tara's light bags. Tara, lagging behind with several nephews, thought the station was more like a hospital; there were so many sick and deformed men sitting listlessly on bundles and trunks. When she caught up with the uncle she found him very angry. Tara and the Bengal Tiger, if he had come, had been put in a four-berth compartment with two others. He read the names of the passengers on the reservation slip above the compartment's door. "They are both men!" he exploded. "I can't allow you to travel under such conditions."

"What nonsense this is!" added the aunt. "Not only are they

men, but on top of that, they're non-Bengalis! *Arré baba!*"

The uncle tried to arrange more proper traveling accommodations, but the air-conditioned coach that night seemed filled with businessmen and one recently married couple who wanted to be together. Tara, anxious to get started on the last lap of her journey home, assured the nervous uncle that he really should not worry, that she would spend both nights on the train sitting up.

The Bombay aunt and the nephews began to cry as they waited for her train to leave. The Bombay uncle became very emotional. He bought her two bars of Cadbury's chocolate, then paid a large tip to the air-conditioned-class attendant so he might give Tara extra care. His entire family entrusted last-minute messages for the relatives in Calcutta. Then the two other occupants appeared, the train began to move slowly, and the aunt, uncle and nephews had to quickly jump off.

She did not wish to study her traveling companions. Her Bombay aunt would have said all Marwaris are ugly, frugal and vulgar, and all Nepalis are lecherous. Tara hoped she had a greater sense of justice toward non-Bengalis. But the gentlemen in the compartment simply did not interest her. The Marwari was indeed very ugly and tiny and insolent. He reminded her of a circus animal who had gotten the better of his master. The Nepali was a fidgety older man with coarse hair. He kept crossing and recrossing his legs and pinching the creases of his pants. Both men, Tara decided, could effortlessly ruin her journey to Calcutta.

Before the train had made its first stop the Marwari and the Nepali were starting to bait each other. It began with a quarrel over luggage space, but Tara feared they were responding to other irritations. She sat surrounded by bedrolls, trunks, old leather suitcases, baskets of fruits, while the Nepali tried to push her Samsonite bag out into the corridor.

"This is too large, lady," he objected. "How you think there'll be room here for that monster?"

"It is small, excuse me," answered the Marwari. "The lady's suitcase is the smallest here. I'll call the attendant this minute if you don't move *your* bags and baggage."

Tara's feelings did not appear to matter at all. Her suitcase had become part of a general irritability. In the end the question of luggage was resolved without the aid of the attendant. The two men piled the pieces in the middle of the floor, making the compartment's washbasin totally inaccessible.

She was frightened by the capacity for anger over trivial encounters. She stared out of the window to avoid watching the night ablutions of her companions. I have returned to dry holes by the sides of railway tracks, she thought, to brown fields like excavations for a thousand homes. I have returned to India.

At Jamnagar the aging "boys" in soiled caterers' turbans called out, "Dinner! Dinner!" The Nepali ordered the English menu. Tara, still close to David's worries, feared diarrhea, jaundice and polluted water. She ordered a Coke. The Marwari, true to his nature, ordered nothing.

After years of airplanes and Greyhound buses Tara felt she should be thrilled to travel in an Indian train. Her mother's brother worked with diesel locomotives and so she had been trained since childhood to think well of the Indian railways. But this time the train ride depressed her. She fretted about David as she sat in the hostile compartment. Perhaps I was stupid to come without him, she thought, even with him rewriting his novel during the vacation. Perhaps I was too impulsive, confusing my fear of New York with homesickness. Or perhaps I was going mad.

The dinner tray arrived at a station where there were monkeys on the train tracks, white monkeys calmly eating by the side of freight cars. The "boy" placed the tray before the Nepali passenger. Mulligatawny soup in a stainless steel bowl, poached eggs, toast, boiled okra and carrots, bread pudding. Then a feckless Coke without a straw for Tara. She pursed her lips around the wet, warm bottle, then suddenly panicked. How long had it lain about, opened? Old worries flooded her, warnings from her mother about VD contracted in public toilets, sinister sexual germs lurking in railway stations.

"I don't want it after all," she said, paying for the Coke. The attendant took the bottle away and drank it in the corridor.

The Nepali traveler looked rather embarrassed to be the only one eating. He smiled vaguely, rubbed his hands on the limp napkin, and started on his soup.

"The Indian menu is hopeless," he commented, sucking in a spoonful of rice floating in yellow liquid. "Madam, are you new here?"

"Yes and no," said Tara, preparing to hide behind a *Time* magazine.

The Marwari stirred in his corner. Now he reminded her of a spider, impassive and calculating. He stood up, and Tara noted dry, goose-pimpled flesh hanging loosely from his bony arms. He reached under his seat for a tiffin carrier propped between bedroll and suitcase. The tiffin carrier consisted of four round brass cans stacked between two brass stems and held together by a wooden handle. She had not seen a tiffin carrier, not even thought of one, in seven years. She wondered if David had ever heard the word.

The Marwari dismantled the carrier and laid the cans side by side on the white leather seat. Around the bottoms of the cans pale yellow rings of moisture began to spread on the leather. There were wilted *chapatis* and four lemon wedges in one container, fried pumpkin and eggplant slices in another, cabbage curry in a third, and homemade yoghurt in the fourth. The spidery little man pointed to his cans like a roadside vendor and tried to tempt Tara to share his "humble and native food, Madam." Again she thought the meal had been turned into a battle by the travelers, that her answer was crucial to both men though her hunger was, to them, quite inconsequential. She accepted a wedge of lemon, sprinkling it with coarse salt, and pleaded fatigue after the long flight from America.

The sharpness of the lemon pulp and the granular taste of salt released in her faint and nostalgic agitations. As a child she had sucked lemon pieces and her mother had worried about her teeth. It'll melt the enamel, she had said, and at thirty you'll be a toothless *buddhi*. Her mother had never been to the dentist. Her grandmother Santana had chewed cane till the night before her death. Cavities they regarded as a white man's disease. Tara herself had been to the dentist only once, at the university clinic in Madison, where she had cried as a team of dental students had peered at, then extracted, her decayed wisdom teeth. The Nepali seemed to have been humiliated by Tara's obvious savoring of the lemon. The caterers' boy had long since gone with the half-eaten tray of English dinner, and he had settled down with a Hindi movie magazine in the center of his bench, careful to remove his shoes before folding his sockless feet under him.

"Meena Kumari will be making a new picture about Goddess Durga," he announced suddenly, baring uneven yellow teeth as if he were anxious to start another bout. When Tara did not respond to this new appeal or challenge, he continued, "I see from your luggage tag you have been to New York. I too am foreign-returned. I am Ratan, not quite but almost *Prince* Ratan, Madam." Tara wondered why he did not mention his last name. "And who, may I ask, sir, are you?"

"P. K. Tuntunwala," answered the spider.

"You mean *the* Tuntunwala?" asked Ratan.

Though she generally scorned heroes, the first night back in India Tara did not mind that the man who had made room for her Samsonite bag should be a National Personage. She had heard the name Tuntunwala as a young woman in Calcutta. So this was P. K. Tuntunwala, Esq., originally of Rajasthan, but now of Bombay, Delhi and Calcutta, perhaps even of Geneva. She had heard men say that he was a corporate fear and a selfish energy. She had not expected him to remind her of a spider.

It was difficult to determine the Marwari's response to the question. His teeth were buried in a *chapati* as he sat, still and malevolent, in his corner.

"I'm Tara Banerjee Cartwright."

"You are so beautiful and you are married to a European, Madam?" The Nepali's question, or charge, went unanswered.

"We might have never met if it hadn't been for the *goon-dahs,*" said Mr. Tuntunwala. "I only fly. But happily this was not the best of times for such action."

The Nepali ignored the Marwari and opened a small scratchy leather attaché case. Again Tara felt there was an undercurrent of venom to his smallest actions. The attaché case was jammed with snapshots. He rifled through them carelessly, spilling some on the seat near his bare feet, and some on the dusty floor.

"I want to show you something," he said, fingers curling around the black and white photographs. "I too have been to England. I know many Europeans. Bertie Russell is my friend. And Greg Peck." He finally found the picture he wanted. "Here is me in lederhosen, and her ladyship my spouse. We're eating lunch in Venice with Greg Peck. He thinks I'm a very interesting man."

It was too dark now to make out the photographed faces. If one of them were to turn on the lights, Tara wondered, would something snap? At St. Blaise's she had learned to humiliate people gently. Now on her way back to Calcutta, the gestures, the tones of voice, the deportment and dismissals that she had forgotten in the States suddenly came back with dizzying assurance. She had not thought that seven years in another country, a husband, a new blue passport could be so easily blotted out. She wanted to tell the two men sparring in the dark that she had done more than eat with movie stars, but that nothing she had thought or done could soften her suspicious nature.

The darkness outside the window deepened, giving Tara time for unhappy self-analysis. For years she had dreamed of this return to India. She had believed that all hesitations, all shadowy fears of the time abroad would be erased quite magically if she could just return home to Calcutta. But so far the return had brought only wounds. First the corrosive hours on Marine Drive, then the deformed beggars in the railway station, and now the inexorable train ride steadily undid what strength she had held in reserve. She was an embittered woman, she now thought, old and cynical at twenty-two and quick to take offense.

Tara could not give shape to the dark scenery outside; to her it seemed merely alien and hostile. Except for vacations in the hills or at seaside resorts, she had rarely been outside Bengal. Now, amid subdued malice in a railway compartment, she thought her father's decision to send her to Vassar had been strangely ruthless, though courageous. There were dry river beds out there in the night, she decided, and dry fields and cracked mud houses on hillocks.

Ratan began to put away his photographs. He looked aggressive but defeated from the start. He was talking very rapidly now as if he believed the logic of malevolence would crush his silent and spidery enemy. He leaned closer to Tara while his faintly regal wife stared dimly out of cellulose eyes from leathered recesses.

"I think you're an especially sensitive person, Madam. I see it in your face, it is so pained and beautiful," he said to Tara, balancing himself on his heels on the white seat. "I am also like that. In fact, I don't mind telling you I have ESP. Bertie and I have talked a lot about ESP. He's interested in my ESP. He has invited me to stay with him whenever I'm in England."

"If I'm not mistaken Bertrand Russell died last year," said Tara.

The man did not seem to hear her. He continued about his extrasensory gift, issuing inarticulate little challenges to the spider in the corner. Tara wondered if she could turn this railway encounter into a story . . . *When I was in Tunla, just before the monsoons* . . . But somehow things were less ironical and manageable than she had expected. These men had desecrated her shrine of nostalgia. David at the airport, stooping and sideburned, seemed far less real than the flat-faced Nepali with extrasensory perception. She watched David's healthy face disappear into the fleshy folds of the Nepali's neck and the spider's body, and she was afraid.

"At the end there will be only a few of us left. You know that, don't you? Just a few of us special people. You will be there. Don't be afraid. I promise. I will see you there. Bertie will be there."

"And Gregory Peck?"

The spider laughed in his corner. Ratan went on and on, his voice, like snowflakes, like applause, concealing the silence of a new intimacy between the National Personage and Tara.

2

HOWRAH STATION took Tara by surprise. The airport in Bombay had at least been clean. The squalor and confusion of Howrah Station outraged her. Coolies in red shirts broke into the compartment and almost knocked her down in an effort to carry her suitcase. The attendant sneezed on her raincoat and offered to wipe up the mess with his dusting rag. A blind beggar who had slipped in and had begun to sing and rattle his cup was thrown bodily out of the train by Tuntunwala.

Then the outrage, the confusion, lifted. She had spotted her parents. "Taramoni, my darling!" her father shouted. Time had not shrunk her parents' bulk. They were fat and authoritative on the platform, soft and sentimental as they rushed to embrace her. They dismissed the coolies and handed her bags to family servants.

The Bengal Tiger was still a handsome man, though long years of dominating relatives and factory hands had blunted the delicacy of his features. His curly black hair was cut very close, exposing two small rolls of fat at the base of the skull.

"You look so tired," pronounced the Bengal Tiger.

"I've been traveling, Daddy," said Tara, though she knew there was no excuse for looking tired in public, not even the fifteen thousand miles she had covered in three sleepless nights.

Her father inspected her, frowning, holding short fingers up to her cheek and chin. "What is this? This is not the same little girl I sent off to Vassar."

"I was only fifteen, Daddy. Have I become old and ugly?"

Tara's mother was embarrassed. "No, no, of course not. How could *you* become ugly?" She herself was a good-looking woman with finely grained skin, and dark brown hair drawn into a gentle knot. Extreme emotion was injurious to beauty, she had taught Tara; but now she was becoming almost emotional.

"But so thin," insisted her father. "Doesn't this fellow feed you?"

"I was fat when I went away, Daddy. It isn't healthy . . ."

"Yes, yes, that's all Mummy and I hear from these new Bengali doctors. I tell them if it was healthy to be thin then Calcutta would be the healthiest city in the world." He shook with sudden, loud laughter. People on the platform turned and smiled.

"Don't just stand around," shouted the Bengal Tiger to his servants. "Get those bags quickly. Where is the driver?"

While the Bengal Tiger turned to shout instructions to the chauffeur, Tara's distant relatives squeezed closer so they could touch her. They had come to the railway station in two small delivery trucks from the tobacco firm. For days they had chattered about welcoming little "Taramoni," whom they claimed to remember vividly. But now that they were actually in front of Tara, they had nothing to say to her. Surrounded by this army of relatives who professed to love her, and by vendors ringing bells, beggars pulling at sleeves, children coughing on tracks, Tara felt completely alone. Only the Bengal Tiger, body half-turned away from her while he shouted instructions, seemed to her real.

The Bengal Tiger had assumed, Tara recalled, a characteristic position. In profile his stomach stuck out extravagantly from the edges of his tropical-weight trousers. Except for the stomach, he was not really a fat man but gave the appearance of being fat.

Tara watched his body turn now left, then right, slicing as it turned through that shy and brutal atmosphere of Howrah Station. For a moment she thought she was going mad. For she felt that the Bengal Tiger, set apart from the smell and noise of the platform, had in her absence moved out of the private world of filial affection. He seemed to have become a symbol for the outside world. He had become a pillar supporting a balcony that had long outlived its beauty and its function.

During those first minutes beside an emptying and hissing train, Tara felt the crowd's reverence for her father draw toward her and then recoil, embarrassed. Awed and vulgar stares scored their triumphs against her. Then the Bengal Tiger was at her side, raising raucous laughs from the crowd, and she felt safer. She caught the sense of occasional sentences he uttered, his explanations of car arrangements, the remarks he had made to her mother at breakfast about the perfect timing of Tara's train, his grave and impersonally tragic revelation that Tara's grandmother had died four years before of a heart attack. All Calcutta, it seemed to her, had been touched by public rages and ideals; and in its ceaseless effort to escape the present, her familiar part of Calcutta had created of the Bengal Tiger its key to a more peaceful world. They leaned on him as naturally as she had. The vacation, she realized, would not be an easy one; every trivial gesture, every tea party or card game would torture her with its suspicions.

"Come along now. Let's not talk of such sad things here. As the lovely lady said, *Que será, será.* What will be, will be. We're all powerless."

So Tara was received by her family on a crowded platform in Howrah Station. The place was too noisy and filthy of course to allow her any insight into the world to which she had returned. In any case she did not excel in insights and intuitions. She did, however, feel the Bengal Tiger was slightly disappointed in her. He had said nothing of course, but then they had never really talked about important things. They had covered up misgivings with loyalty and trust. She could depend on him to protect her now that she was back within his reach; yet the certainty that he would remain loyal to her in spite of deficiencies depressed her. Calcutta had already begun to exert its darkness over her, she thought.

3

AFTER THE JOURNEY from Bombay, Tara rested for a full forty-eight hours. Her parents' house on Camac Street was designed to be restful. All anxiety and unpleasantness was prevented from entering the premises by two men in khaki suits. These men were the *durwans*, the gate-keepers. On their breast pockets, embroidered in red, they wore her father's initials. The men were proud of the uniform, which they knew would be taken away from them in the event of dismissal or resignation.

When an unfamiliar visitor approached the Banerjees' front gates, he was carefully inspected by the two *durwans*. The *durwans* relied solely on their scrutiny: hard, embarrassing, almost arrogant. For though they were armed with light nightsticks and curved daggers, they were gentle souls, and would have been afraid to use their weapons. The visitor who handled himself competently in this first trial was then escorted by the younger *durwan* up the semicircular driveway to the carport. On either side of the drive was a large and aggressive lawn, kept green by a full-time *mali* and his six-year-old son. The *mali's* job was to make sure there were enough flowers for the daily religious rituals, and for the thirty-odd vases and bowls scattered throughout the house.

The lawn was rarely used. It was too hot during the day to sit outdoors, and in any case Tara's mother, who suffered from headaches, preferred the darkness of the air-conditioned interior. The Banerjees would perhaps have liked to sip their cocktails outdoors, but they were inhibited by their good breeding. It was considered impolite to eat in full view of others, and though there were high brick walls studded with spikes and shards of glass, they were afraid someone might spy from an upstairs window.

At the carport the visitor was handed over by the *durwan* to the bearer, who then escorted him to the hall, verandah, or formal drawing room. To enter the hall, one had to pass through gigantic double doors, hung with coir blinds. The blinds were sprayed with rose-scented cold water on the hour. These doors remained open all day, but were chained and padlocked in four separate places at ten every night when the family retired. A few servants who had been with the family for at least eight years, and who had business in the house early in the morning, were allowed to sleep in the main building. The rest of the staff, their wives, children, cousins and occasional friends, lived in the servants' quarters behind the house.

The hall was eclectically furnished. Italian marble tables, and mahogany tables in the shapes of hearts, clubs, diamonds and spades, occupied the dingy corners. On two heart-shaped tables stood enormous ebony elephants. On the high-ceilinged walls hung framed photographs of earlier Banerjees. From legend one knew these Banerjees had noble faces, that some had been photographed in yogic positions, bare chests girdled by Brahminic thread. But the grime on the glass made these facts impossible to verify. As a child Tara had often amused herself, especially in the rainy season, by scratching the grease with her long fingernails. But she could only reach the toes and ankles of the photographed men. In a poorly lit corner hung one headless tiger skin. It had been acquired by Tara's maternal grandfather, a hunter of moderate renown, before he had given up big-game hunting. Tara's father was not a sportsman.

The living room was filled with imported furniture — heavy,

dark, incongruous pieces whose foreignness had been only slightly mitigated by brilliantly colored Indian upholstery. In built-in glass cabinets, expecting to be admired, were large, tarnished silver cups that Tara and her father before her had won in annual debating championships.

"I like glass cabinets," Tara's mother had often said. "We're honest people. We have nothing to hide." She obviously had the courage of her convictions, for she did not try to hide the one tiny cup, a fifth prize, that the Bengal Tiger had won in the egg-and-teaspoon race on the Banerjee & Thomas [Tobacco] Co. Sports Day.

On the days the *mali* performed his work, clumps of tropical flowers sprang from the vases. They had been arranged by Tara's mother, who had been trained in the minor decorative arts, to sing well, play the sitar, supervise cooks, and above all to please her husband and her in-laws. There was a great deal of dust everywhere. The sweepers cleaned regularly, morning and late afternoon, but they were not expected to rid the room of dust. There were occasional ants on the floor, large, black and indolent. Insects were not a source of embarrassment.

An old-fashioned wooden door, armed with steel bolts, hooks, and chains, draped with diaphanous pink net curtains, gave access to a spacious verandah. As a child, surprisingly shy in spite of the solidity of her background, Tara had found the verandah the most comfortable place in the house. She had loved the chalky whiteness of its walls, pillars and grilles. Against this whiteness exploded bougainvilleas, purple and vermilion, hibiscus, marigolds, full-bodied dahlias, cascades of golden laburnum. These flowers were not carefully contained in vases or bowls, but grew, almost in spite of the *mali*, in pots lining the wide edges of the balcony railing. They flowered in insolent detachment from the landscaped garden below, sharing nothing with the cut flowers in the living room so pleasantly arranged, nothing with the Banerjee family and their servants who loved flowers. They grew as if they had independent destinies.

Dwarfed by the flowers were two deep canvas easy chairs — reminiscent of the order and ease of the British days without its bitterness or alarms — four green rattan chairs, a table, and a low divan. Pale brown lizards slept on the walls of this verandah, and once Tara had seen a chameleon among the flowers.

The only extraordinary equipment in the verandah was a Sears and Roebuck garden swing, sold to the Banerjees by a departing librarian of the local USIS. The swing had been redone by the family tailor in green and yellow brocade. Even the awning was made from silk brocade. Though the swing was no doubt intended to be hammered into the earth, it had adapted itself to Bengal Tiger Banerjee's wishes, and settled firmly into the marble floors of the verandah. And here was the tableau she suddenly remembered: in the center of the garden swing, with his wife at his side (she suffered his drinking grimly), a servant massaging his tired feet, would sit the Bengal Tiger, confident and sentimental, over his nightly pegs of local Scotch.

After seven years abroad, after extraordinary turns of destiny that had swept her from Calcutta to Poughkeepsie, and Madison, and finally to a two-room apartment within walking distance of Columbia, strange turns that had taught her to worry over a dissertation on Katherine Mansfield, the plight of women and racial minorities, Tara was grateful to call this restful house home.

The house on Camac Street began to exercise its hypnosis on her. New York, she thought now, had been exotic. Not because it had laundromats and subways. But because there were policemen with dogs prowling the underground tunnels. Because girls like her, at least almost like her, were being knifed in elevators in their own apartment buildings. Because students were rioting about campus recruiters and far-away wars rather than the price of rice or the stiffness of final exams. Because people were agitated over pollution. The only pollution she had been warned against in Calcutta had been caste pollution. New York was certainly extraordinary, and it had driven her to despair. On days she had thought she could not possibly survive, she had shaken out all her silk scarves, ironed them and hung them to make the apartment more "Indian." She had curried hamburger desperately till David's stomach had protested.

"I can think of a perfect ad for Alka-Seltzer . . ." he had begun, and she had blushed at her own inconsiderateness.

She had burned incense sent from home (You must be careful about choosing brands when it comes to incense, her mother always said), till the hippie neighbors began to take an undue interest in her.

Now she was home, surrounded by imported furniture, in a house that filtered sunlight and unwelcome guests through an elaborate system of coir blinds, rose-water sprays, *durwans,* bearers, heavy doors, locks, chains and hooks. She was home in a class that lived by Victorian rules, changed decisively by the exuberance of the Hindu imagination. Now she was in a city that took for granted most men were born to suffer, others to fall asleep during committee meetings of the chamber of commerce. She was among the ordinary and she felt rested.

While Tara sat in an easy chair, trying hard to relax and recover, a vision, not necessarily benevolent, hidden by flowers and lizards, smiled at her audacity, then quickly retired.

4

ON HER THIRD DAY in Calcutta, Tara's mother took her to visit the relatives.

"They will be so offended if we delay any more."

"But I'm still tired," Tara objected.

"Take us to Southern Avenue first," the mother said to the chauffeur. "Poor Jharna must be given top priority."

"Yes, *memsahib*."

"She's had such a hard life. Why does *Bhagwan* permit such cruelty? Your Uncle Sachin died of cancer, and that child of hers is clubfooted."

"So it *was* cancer, after all?"

"Yes. From Jharna's we'll look at saris at New Market. We'll keep the rest of the relatives for another day."

Aunt Jharna and her children lived on the middle floor of a shabby and malevolent building. There were a cabinetmaker and a palmist's clinic on the ground floor; Aunt Jharna lived on the second; a tenant's consumptive family on the third.

The chauffeur let out the two women, and then ran forward to ring the doorbell. There was really no need to ring. A boy of about fourteen in short *khaki* pants was standing at the front door.

"*Namaste, Didimoni,*" the boy said, with folded hands. "*Memsahib* is waiting for you upstairs."

The chauffeur returned to the car, flicking it arrogantly with a yellow feather duster, protecting its luster from the fingerprints of neighborhood beggars, while the women followed the servant boy. They went across a tiny inner courtyard, up an open, steep staircase to a spacious foyer. The foyer, partly enclosed by walls and partly by long canvas hangings, was filled with smoke fumes. In the pungent grayness Tara could barely make out her aunt, who was seated on the floor, fanning a clay incense burner. A little girl in a printed cotton dress sat on a rattan chair, and dangled her bare feet above the smoking incense.

"*Didi,* how good of you to come," Aunt Jharna said. "I'll be through with this very soon." Aunt Jharna was an angular woman with a sallow complexion that passed for fairness in India. She continued to fan with an elaborately decorated hand fan, and when that did not produce results quickly enough she blew into the incense burner till her cheeks looked almost transparent and about to burst.

"Mother," said the little girl, "it hurts."

Tara wondered what hurt, the feet or the smoke. She was revolted. Not so much by the legs, absurdly misshapen, but by the scene, by the arrangement of child, mother and incense burner. The fumes, perfumed, opaque, holy, swirled around the women. Tara knew, from remembered scraps of her mother's letters, those feet had pleaded before London-trained Bengali surgeons, Seventh Day Adventists, dead Moslem saints, and tribal faith healers.

"Have you tried plaster casts and special shoes, Aunt Jharna?" asked Tara, wanting to spare herself the humiliation of the scene.

"You think you are too educated for this, don't you?" Aunt Jharna laughed with a quiet violence. "You have come back to make fun of us, haven't you? What gives you the right? Your American money? Your *mleccha* husband?"

Tara heard the embarrassed jingle of her mother's gold bracelets.

"Jharna, don't work yourself up again. She was trying to be helpful, and you know that."

"They're all alike, these college girls, they think they are too educated for us."

If it had not been for a strange, unexpected little twinge called love, Tara would have screamed and run out of the house to the safety of the car.

"Why do you despise our ways? That's what comes of going to a school like St. Blaise's."

How does the foreignness of the spirit begin? Tara wondered. Does it begin right in the center of Calcutta, with forty ruddy Belgian women, fat foreheads swelling under starched white headdresses, long black habits intensifying the hostility of the Indian sun? The nuns had taught her to inject the right degree of venom into words like "common" and "vulgar." They had taught her *The Pirates of Penzance* in singing class, and "If I should die, think only this of me —" for elocution.

Did the foreignness drift inward with the winter chill at Vassar, as she watched the New York snow settle over new architecture, blonde girls, Protestant matrons, and Johnny Mathis? Or was it not till Madison that she first suspected the faltering of the heart?

Madison had been unbearable that first winter. Then one chilly morning in the spring of 1967 David Cartwright had thrust himself through the closing doors of an elevator. "It's been a violent day," he had said, and Tara had fallen in love with him before the elevator ride was over. It was silly to ask oneself questions of the heart, Tara decided. There were no definite points in time that one could turn to and accuse or feel ashamed of as the start of this dull strangeness.

The smoke had made her drowsy. She wanted to pull apart the canvas hangings, so that thin rays of sunlight could insinuate themselves through the tall, narrow buildings and the incense fumes.

"It's too late anyway," Tara said, trying to apologize.

"Why do you hate us?" Aunt Jharna demanded.

If she were more passionate she might have said, I don't hate you, I love you, and the miserable child, the crooked feet, the smoking incense holder, I love you all.

The servant saved the situation. He brought in two plates of sweetmeats, set them on low gate-legged tables, and said, with obvious pride, in English, "Good app'tite, *Didimoni!*"

The sweetmeats, circular, white and stolid, rested on heavy blue-ringed china plates on the dusty, filigreed table tops.

"Eat, eat, *Didimoni*," encouraged the servant from the doorway. "Don't be shy. Treat this house like your own."

"The eight-*anna* size *rosogolla* becomes smaller and harder every week," sighed Aunt Jharna. "So many sweetmeat-makers have committed suicide because of the sugar shortage." She had regained her composure of the repressed, and was quietly putting away the incense.

Fearing another attack from her aunt, Tara ate quickly, digging the light aluminum teaspoon into the heart of the *rosogolla*. As Tara and her mother were being shown out by the servant boy, he said, "She is bad-tempered after each fast, and the fasts get longer and longer for *missybaba's* legs. But she's been a mother to me, no, she has been a goddess."

5

ON THE ROOF of the Catelli-Continental, dwarfed by two potted magnolias, sat Joyonto Roy Chowdhury, owner of tea estates in Assam. He was dressed in a blazer with shiny buttons, crisp white trousers, and sockless sandals. A cane, crooked and gnarled, lay on the table next to the morning newspaper. In his youth Joyonto must have been startlingly handsome. Even now he had the deportment of the handsome young. But a habitual and deep distrust gave his face a slightly malicious sneer. It was a face that had known restlessness or failure, the face of a statesman whose country had let him down.

Joyonto's years of distrust had been preceded by many more years of ignorance. Till recently he had gone about his family's business without any distractions. He had inspected his tea plantations, attended annual trade meetings in London, interviewed young trainees from the management schools, consoled widows, placed the sons of faithful employees, and in short, done all the things expected of him and his class. Like his friends in those peaceful times, he had read the Vedas in translation, executed simple lotus positions, consulted astrologers for auspicious occasions and had even fasted on serious provocation. He had suffered no mysteries, and certainly no revelations.

Then one morning very early in the sixties, late for an appointment with a local tobacco magnate (the astrologer had prophesied failure anyway), he had entered the Catelli for the first time. He had taken the self-service lift up to the open-air café, ordered an espresso, and there on the roof of the hotel, alone among giant flowerpots and undersized waiters, he had been struck by the awesome failure of his love. It was a curious and sudden self-judgment, provoked by no incident at the Catelli, no snub or threat, unless the stench and cries of Chowringhee Avenue can be taken for accusations by decent men.

After that morning of revelation, Joyonto Roy Chowdhury returned to the Catelli every day to order coffee that he rarely drank and to reflect on the deep consequences of a fate he did not understand. He was neither hurt nor angered by the knowledge of personal failure; it merely directed his attention to public questions. He thought his own destiny was but a faint shadow of what Calcutta could expect. And so, like the city, he watched the ugly decay from his hotel perch.

In time the sidewalks beneath Joyonto grew restless with refugees from East Bengal and Tibet. Rioters became insolent. Powerful landowners were at first tormented, later beheaded. Businessmen padlocked their factories and snuck off like ghosts to richer provinces. Housewives cried at night, or retreated into screaming hate.

6

ON A BRIGHT Monday morning, bare feet withdrawn from sandals and blazer tightly buttoned, Joyonto sat at his usual corner in the open-air café of the Catelli-Continental and leaned over the sun-warmed edge of the balcony to survey Chowringhee Avenue below. On the grassy *maidan* across the street two small boys were running with a kite. A group of beggar women sat under a tree, drying their long black hair. A dog wearing a garland of marigolds panted in his sleep beside a trident-carrying holy man. Farther off middle-aged men in shorts were playing soccer with a soft ball.

"Coffee, *sahib?*" asked the waiter, but did not wait for the old man's answer. Joyonto looked down at his toes, very fair and cracked around the heels, then was distracted by a swirl of pale cotton saris and dark worsted pants advancing toward his table. The legs, the multicolored sandals and black oxfords came nearer and nearer, and the old man panicked and took refuge in a crazy game of words. He liked to call the game his "short-sighted visionary small talk." *Truth is a head on a stake.* The feet had passed his table. But he persevered with his game. *Nostrils are lined with the sourness of death. The sun this year is evil.* Six men and women had joined two tables close to him, and were settling down now in a flurry of pale colors. *Sleep chars the body.* The newcomers began to distract him with their loud talk and gestures; there was no longer any pleasure or safety for him in words though he tried to return to them again and again. *We are the sum of our cities and houses.* The effort only fatigued him, so he abandoned the game of phrases and eavesdropped instead on the elegant newcomers.

For almost an hour he watched and listened to the young people, having nothing to do or say himself. The city had dried the blood in his body, and now he had lost even his curious phrases. *On the skeletons of cows skyscrapers will rise.* But he knew it was no use, the new guests had disturbed his surface of words, and now he must yield to their terrible presence. He thought they were very much as he had been in his twenties, and the thought frightened him even more than he had expected. The young men and women reminded him of trapped gazelles though they were confident, handsome and brashly opinionated as they joked across the aqua tables. They spoke mainly in English, occasionally changing to Bengali in midsentence, almost always in exclamations, favoring "How dare you!" and "What nonsense!" He heard them list with enthusiasm movies they had seen or parties they had recently attended. As he rubbed his cracked and dirt-grained heels against the aqua legs of the table, Joyonto heard their conversation alight on imported gadgets, on stereos, transistors, blenders and percolators; each foreign word was treated with a holy reverence. When they touched current events he thought it was mainly to show their familiarity with *Time* magazine or *Reader's Digest.* The real Calcutta, the thick laughter of brutal men, open dustbins, warm and dark where carcasses were sometimes discarded, did not exist. He knew Calcutta would not be as kind to them as it had been to him.

He tried to comfort himself again with his game of phrases, scurrying desperately between words, long ones and skinny ones, slow ones and sharp ones, to build his defense. *Hill stations are cavities. Smell. Prick the night and see it swell. Cuts and nicks that house insects. Dogs feed on curried cabbage. Smell, smell.* Then a young woman walked in, a sober or subdued young woman, who was greeted with extraordinary emotion by the six newcomers, and Joyonto turned slowly on his aqua seat to watch her.

Luminous Brahmin children must be saved, Joyonto said.

7

"MY! IT'S SO WEIRD to have you back here, Tara!"

"I can't believe you've ever been away. She hasn't changed one bit, isn't that just too much!"

"What nonsense, she wasn't always so glamorous! I mean look at her short hair and all. And that sari! It *has* to be from New York!"

They studied Tara with obsessive attention as if she were not present. They seemed perfectly relaxed as they discussed her hair, the shade of her lipstick, her sunglasses; Tara was startled at their tremendous capacity for surfaces. She sat in their midst, cowed and nervous while her silence drove them to more indelicate, more damaging remarks about her appearance. Then having tired of that, they moved lightly to other favorite topics, leaving Tara miserably acquiescent.

"Tara, don't you think Calcutta's changed unbelievably? I mean can you recognize this place at all?"

"Wait till you've seen a riot here. They're really something!"

"What nonsense! She better not listen to you people. She's an *Americawali* now, she won't know you're joking."

"They raided five schools last week. What do you mean?"

"Stop, stop, *arré baba!* Are you going to fight?"

"Talking of schools, Tara should see how St. Blaise's has changed! Those nuns are taking in Marwaris by the dozens!"

"Really, everything, I mean just everything's gone down horribly. Everything stinks nowadays."

It was hard for Tara to respond to the changes in the city and at St. Blaise's. Her friends had warmed to their subject. They were locked in a private world of what should have been and they relished every twinge of resentment and defeat that time had reserved for them. Tara cut through insulating layers of American experiences till she could visualize again Mother Peter entering a classroom, rosary muffled by her habit, to trap violaters of the silence rule. She thought at this moment David was probably sitting in his lumpy green chair, surrounded by quarterlies and radical journals and missing her very much.

"I'm telling you at the first hint of riot, Tara's going to run away to America, no?"

"How dare you suggest she'll run away? At least Calcutta isn't uncultured like Bombay!"

Some instinct or intuition told her to stay away from these people who were her friends, only more, much more, for they were shavings of her personality. She feared their tone, their omissions, their aristocratic oneness. They had asked her about the things she brought back, had admired her velours jumpsuit and electric lady-shaver, but not once had they asked about her husband. (Of course I didn't bring *him* back, she thought.) Seven years ago she had worn a garland of roses and gardenias and a yoghurt spot on her forehead for luck, and had taken a plane to America. Seven years ago she had played with these friends, done her homework with Nilima, briefly fancied herself in love with Pronob, debated with Reena at the British Council.

"Calcutta's going to the dogs. No question about it. It's going to the left-of-leftists. It's going communist."

"Oh, don't even mention that word. It reminds me of Mother Xavier on her knees, trying to save the world."

"You know, I can't bring myself to read any Dostoevski," said Nilima.

"But I don't think he was a —," said Tara.

"So what, he was a Russian, wasn't he?"

"I didn't blame the leaders," said Pronob. "It's the workers that disgust me. We pay medical insurance for them, pension plans, education taxes for their kids, and what do they do? Turn round and *gherao* us."

"*Gherao*," repeated Tara. "I read about it in the States."

"You may have read about it, dear girl, but you can't possibly know what it is."

"If these *gheraos* continue, we'll all have to move Bombay-side. What a ghastly prospect!"

"Do you know what they did at Pronob's factory?"

"Please, please. I don't want to talk about it," he said with a worldly flourish. "Certainly not in front of these ladies."

"Come on, Pronob, be a sport," said Tara.

"Well, if you feel you can take it. These *goondahs* surrounded us for eighteen hours. There was no food, no water, no nothing. When we tried to get water, do you know what these comm ——, left-of-leftists did? They sent in a Coke bottle filled with . . ." he hesitated. Conversations about bathrooms were not permitted in Calcutta's westernized society.

"I understand," said Tara.

"A damn lot of cheek I call it, a damn lot of gall." The young man quivered with passion.

What were they to do? Tara wondered. Should they leave for Bombay and let the rich Marwaris fight it out with the *goondahs?* The Marwaris were less vulnerable. They belched in public, they wiped their noses on their shirt-sleeves, they were insensitive. They could stand up to the communists. But what of the poor Bengalis, the descendants of Hari Lal Banerjee who had inherited, not earned, their wealth, their frailties, their conscience? Bombay, she knew, was no answer. It was like Chekhov, she felt, yearning for Moscow but staying.

Tara had, perhaps unfortunately, allowed literature to disturb the placid surface of her life. At Vassar she had heard first of existentialism, followed closely by postexistentialism. That first winter in Poughkeepsie she had been given Sartre and Camus, Rilke and Mann, and the Joyce beyond *Dubliners,* and her closed little heart had been flooded. She had even begun writing stories about Calcutta based on the style and subtleties of Joyce and she had stopped only when they had become too easy, too obvious. How could she tell her friends that Bombay was no answer, that people in Bombay snickered at Tagore, and that the girls there wore skirts and were trained for office work? They would have to learn to endure *gheraos* and Coke bottles filled with urine and vulgar men leering at them. But how could she explain the bitterness of it to David, who would have laughed at her friends and wished them luck as refugees and beggars in Shambazar? What would he care? He'd laughed when she described Rajah's burial in a children's cemetery, been disgusted that a servant had been kept just to feed and walk a dog.

"It's all so very different," Tara said. "And it's going to be a lot more different . . . and tragic."

"Don't be silly!" Pronob retorted. "We've got to beat this nonsense out of the system. Purge our factories of unions and things like that."

Tara was not familiar with unions, labor demands or picket

lines. Only once when the Bengal Tiger was young had there been a strike and lockout at Banerjee & Thomas [Tobacco] Co., Ltd. There had been no melodrama then that Tara could remember. No petrol-filled Coke bottles, no vulgar exchanges. Only the Bengal Tiger's moving rhetoric. In the end her father's words, intense, hard and sincere, had set him above the other directors. For her father the strike had been a triumph. He had been challenged and he had brought order to his men. But now the shapes of factories and men were different. An appetite for the grotesque had taken over the city. There was no room for heroic oratory in Calcutta; Tara understood that from Pronob's anecdote.

As if to confirm Tara's fears, Pronob shouted, "Come on, you people. Let's be happy-go-lucky, please. Tara, why are you looking so somber?"

Joyonto Roy Chowdhury, two tables away, observed to himself that these men and women, so tall, so straight and elegant, were the last pillars of his world. They did not know or care that a revolution was on its way. They were content to sit at the Catelli and rage against the vulgarity of small riots. He marveled at their dedication to the trivial. Addicted to phrases and words, he said: *Breath is demolished like green rust. History is a tramline uprooted in Shambazar.* He thought they deserved to die as they called out comic and angry eulogies for a wretched Calcutta — all except the luminous girl who sat like a grateful outcaste. And Joyonto, the old player of phrases, the man who had felt clutches of hurt in the whitest folds of his brain, vowed to seek out this girl and preserve her from the others.

8

TARA'S MOTHER, Arati, was a saintly woman. At least, she was given to religious dreams. Her religious dreams were not holy enough to turn her hair white overnight (as had happened to her grandmother once in Pachapara), but they were adequately religious. She could tell, for instance, through Kali or Mother Durga, which pregnant relative would be blessed with a male child, which niece or nephew would pass the final matriculation examination, or which out-of-town acquaintance would suddenly arrive unannounced for a month's visit. Once, in younger days, she had dreamed of Vishnu buried deep in the ground, crying to her for help, and her father's workmen, digging according to her instructions, had disinterred two Vishnu statues.

As a saintly woman, Tara's mother spent a great deal of time in the prayer room. To reach the family's prayer room, she had to pass through a dressing room, a bathroom and Tara's study. She managed to leave behind a considerable religious residue in each of these rooms. In the dressing room Arati stored her precious jewelry and life-insurance policies in three fireproof eight-foot steel cabinets. She called the life-insurance policies "those things," and looked after them with a zealot's fastidiousness. "Those things" had caused her great pain. Her mother-in-law had accused her of trying to kill her son. Widowed in-laws had humiliated her by giving her the boniest piece of curried fish at public feasts. A great-uncle-in-law had forced her to choose between "those things" and the affections of the joint-family system. Arati had chosen allegiance to life-insurance policies and had moved to the house on Camac Street with her steel cabinets and her husband.

Tara, trying to explain and share her background with David

(he had so little, just his divorced mother in Boston whom he called infrequently) had found "those things" embarrassing. She had feared a foreigner would not understand such devotion to insurance terms and payments. It was the one detail in her life she had deliberately misrepresented.

"My mother's a very modern woman," she had said to David. "She believes in those things. And wills and all that. She thinks of them as PROGRESS. I mean things were really bad for Bengali women, it's not funny."

The saintly mother also spent an unreasonable amount of time in the bathroom next to the dressing room. Taking three baths a day was a principle with her. These baths were carefully timed, and on the occasions the Palta Waterworks stopped the water supply for a few hours, Arati was devastated. This bathroom was in the "English style," which meant it was equipped with an erratic commode, bathtub and shower in addition to the many pails, cisterns and drains of the native bathroom. There were three other "Indian style" bathrooms in the house.

"Why three baths a day for God's sake?" David had asked.

"Would *you* like to touch God when you're all horribly sweaty and dirty?" Really, there was no end to David's naive questions.

Arati's religiosity had encountered no difficulty in Tara's study; Hari Lal's granddaughter Arati was incapable of defeat. She had merely diversified her religiosity. She had selected with worshipful pride chairs, bookcases and desks (there were two); she had spent hours choosing and cooking carp's brain and spinach so Tara might improve her intelligence. Wooden bookcases filled with titles like *Westward Ho, Kon-Tiki,* and *Seven Years in Tibet,* all prizes won at St. Blaise's, lined three walls of the study. Against the fourth wall stood a tall metal bookshelf that had been requisitioned from the reading room of the Banerjee &

Thomas [Tobacco] Co., Ltd. This held the school textbooks Tara had used since the age of three when she had been sent to St. Blaise's in earnest. Tara's mother had read every single book on those shelves.

The study led to the prayer room where Arati was at her best. Long after, on homesick afternoons at Vassar, or after misunderstandings with David, or when things went badly between her and Katherine Mansfield, she thought of Camac Street, especially of her mother on a tiny Mirzapur rug, voluminous hips outspread, praying to rows of gods and goddesses.

"It's hard to explain," she had said to the foreign student adviser at Vassar. "I just can't pray here. It doesn't come. Do you know what I mean?"

And the foreign student adviser, who had not known what she meant, had invited her to worship with her at the nearest Episcopalian church every Sunday.

The prayer room was bright, airy and curtainless. Since there was very little furniture in the room, it looked much larger than it really was. Its floor was of white marble, streaked gently with gray. When the morning sun rushed in through the windows, unimpeded by curtains, the floor seemed to dance like waves. The wall farthest from Tara's study supported a marble platform, a sentimental birthday gift from the Bengal Tiger to his religious wife. The Banerjees were serious about birthdays. On this platform stood five small hand-carved tables, their workmanship almost hidden by silk tablecloths. And on these tables were brass and silver deities wearing fresh garlands.

A fortnight after her return to India Tara sat in this room while her mother dusted the icons with affectionate care. If her mother's mind was mainly on God, Tara's was with David's letter, which had arrived earlier that day. David wrote that he had bought two or three books on India and that he would read them if his own writing went badly; that the fifth chapter of his novel was proving tedious; that this summer there weren't too many people he knew around; that Susie Goldberg was now peevish over sexism but still capable of occasional charm. A procession of poorly recalled phrases from David's letter moved about the room and was set on fire by the morning sun, charring the precise order and meaning of his words.

So David had bought books on India. This innocent information enraged Tara. She thought the letter was really trying to tell her that he had not understood her country through her, that probably he had not understood her either. Congenitally suspicious, she turned to David's remarks about Susie Goldberg, who Tara now slowly remembered had her rather charming moments. Tara sensed the beginnings of a long headache that was just fastening itself to her neck and eyeballs. David should have theorized instead about politics and literature. After all he was always trying to educate her, always telling her the names of obscure congresssmen and senators, and buying her paperbacks that she concealed in kitchen drawers. Now that David had confessed his weaknesses, his troubles with his novel, Susie Goldberg's occasional charm, Tara was afraid he no longer wanted to make her over to his ideal image, that he no longer loved her.

Once Tara had admitted this monstrous fear, other suspicions and questions quickly appeared. Perhaps her mother, sitting serenely before God on a tiny rug, no longer loved her either. After all Tara had willfully abandoned her caste by marrying a foreigner. Perhaps her mother was offended that she, no longer a real Brahmin, was constantly in and out of this sacred room, dipping like a crow. She thought her mother had every right to be wary of aliens and outcastes. Once when the local Rotary Club had sent them an Australian religious fanatic for a fortnight, Arati had resorted to mild deceit to keep him out of the prayer room.

"How to explain our God to these Europeans?" Arati had said at the time. To Tara's mother all white men were Europeans and she trusted them only when they were in their proper place. Now Tara saw herself as that unwelcome Australian. Still pained by the odd scraps from David's letter, disturbed by the authentic religious emotions of her mother, she thought it best to go away.

"Don't leave," her mother said, swiveling slightly on her tiny carpet but not breaking the rhythm of her Sanskrit prayers.

For a moment all caution against insults and hurts left Tara. She was moved. She wanted to make some lighthearted rejoinder — "I wouldn't dream of leaving," or something of the sort — but no words would come to her, so she offered with signs to grind the sandalwood paste for the morning's rituals.

"Thank you," whispered her mother, then leaned forward on her knees to offer flowers to a silver icon that Uncle Pomegranate had brought back from a business trip to Gujarat.

When the sandalwood paste had been ground Tara scraped it off the slimy stone tablet with her fingers and poured it into a small silver bowl. But she could not remember the next step of the ritual. It was not a simple loss, Tara feared, this forgetting of prescribed actions; it was a little death, a hardening of the heart, a cracking of axis and center. But her mother came quickly with the relief of words.

"If you've finished making that thing, dear, why don't you just go ahead and bathe Shiva."

"I was just getting ready to do that."

She took down the Shiva-*lingam* from its perch on a table. It was coal black and five inches high, a stone cylindrical protrusion above a stone flower. She thought it looked quite jaunty.

With two fingers she dropped some sandalwood paste on the tip of the protrusion and watched it slide down and splash against the black petals of the flower. She did it again and again, savoring the feel of cold paste and stone, then returned the Shiva-*lingam* to its rightful place on the table.

Tara thought a Hindu was always set apart by his God. The icons before her seemed so exuberant on the silk tablecloths that she wanted to rely on them. In her childhood these icons had worn gold ornaments, tiny 22 karat necklaces and anklets that she had dusted clean with cotton balls. But her mother had donated the ornaments to the Camac Street Ladies' Club Brave Jawan Fund during a border skirmish. It was impossible to explain to a foreigner the extraordinariness of this sacrifice. In Madison, Tara had once read a letter from home to her roommate from Hokkaido, and the girl had giggled loudly. It had been a touching letter, she now recalled.

We're doing our best for the brave *jawans* [her mother had written in Bengali]. We have just started the Camac Street Emergency Ladies' Club and Brave Jawan Fund, and I've been chosen [unanimously] president. We're making bandages from old saris every afternoon (2 P.M.–4 P.M.). Don't worry. We have Patton tanks and many Bengali captains and generals. We'll be successful. Write me more about your studies. I'm sure Goddess Saraswati will make you famous and a doctorate soon. I've told your grandmother (paternal) that I may not have sons like her, but my one daughter is equal to ten sons. I shall pray to Saraswati for success in your exams. On Saraswati Pujah day remember to wear something yellow, she has always looked after you before.

Tara, who remembered all insults, who allowed grudges to ferment till they were unbearable, had never forgiven the girl from Hokkaido. She had continued to room with her, tolerating her only for her efficiency in killing mice.

She wondered how David would react if he could see her that instant.

Her mother clapped her hands, and a line of servants' children entered the room. They arranged themselves against the far wall, quiet and alert, like a row of sandalwood monkeys. Tara's mother asked them questions about their school, their marble games, their sick cousins and brothers as she sliced bananas and oranges and placed them in neat designs on tiny silver plates.

"Song time now," Arati said finally.

The children began to sing. Their voices were harsh and unformed. Tara's first impulse was to clap her hands over her ears; she had not expected such harshness from children. The rough notes and mispronounced names of God mingled dangerously with the sun and incense smoke of the prayer room.

> Raghupati Raghava Rajaram
> Patita Pavana Sitaram

Tara wanted to sing too, hoping the words, the repetition would stave off the madness that curled under the pungent sunlight. She thought the walls of her mind were caving in like black tenement buildings in Shambazar. The children near Tara were screaming now, making each *Raghupati* and *Raghava* crackle, eyeing the fruits offered to the icons on silver plates. Their bright animal-eyes darted from little table to table. A liveliness or greed settled on the children and quickened their song. Tara had not thought that holy names could seem so abrasive.

Then the singing stopped as suddenly as it had begun, leaving Tara unappeased and irritable. The children were making their *pronams* before the icons, their little bottoms turned up in the air, foreheads touching the floor.

"Time for *prasad*," said Tara's mother. "No pushing and shoving please. You know that there's quite enough for all." Fairly and skillfully she divided the oranges and bananas till the last drying slice had disappeared. Some of the children exchanged *prasad* with each other, clawing and snatching; others tied their share in dirty handkerchiefs to carry back to their parents.

"Tonight we'll have extra special *bhajan*. Come back tonight. Come and sing again." Then Arati turned to Tara and added softly, "It will really be extra special if you come. Very fine *bhajan*."

Was her mother crying? Tara wondered. Or had her eyelids always been so gray? She was still a very beautiful woman, and reasonably young. If she had tried, Tara might have calculated Arati's age within five years. But it was inauspicious to know exactly. Long waves of brownish-black hair hung down her back and curled on the floor near her hips. The face was perfectly oval. And sad, Tara thought, in spite of the promised *bhajan*. As a child, Tara remembered, she had sung *bhajans* in that house. She had sat on a love seat beside a very holy man with a limp and had sung *Raghupati Raghava Rajaram*. But that had been a very long time ago, before some invisible spirit or darkness had covered her like skin.

"You will try?"

It was a simple request to share piety with her family. But Tara hid behind flippant remarks, dragging up half-forgotten invitations to parties and charity carnivals as defenses against her mother's request. Both mother and daughter grew nervous, their nervousness visible like monsoon mildew. Outside the heaviness of noon heat had lightened, though afternoon and coolness were still hours away. Tara knew that in the end she would not stay. She could hear the servants' children in the garden below, probably helping their fathers or uncles weed and rake. There were occasional barks from a tired dog, no doubt a *pariah* the children had brought in without telling their parents.

There were more tired barks, pale screams, the soft sounds of slaps, and finally the customary quiet settled over Camac Street. "I really wish I could stay," Tara said.

9

THERE WERE MANY PARTIES in honor of Tara's return. Many teas, many dinners hosted by friends to convince her Calcutta could be as much fun as her New York or Madison. Some of these were written up in the *Feminine Weekly* and the *Ladies of Calcutta Journal*. It was quite evident to people who cared about such things that the city's westernized high society had fallen in love with the Bengali young woman from the States.

The celebrations in her honor frightened Tara. These celebrations were very proper, very lavish in fact, involving rented canopies, caterers' men, nasty young ladies whispering in the garden while poets recited their Sassoonesque verse.

At first Tara had looked forward to these parties. She had rushed to Pronob's or Reena's so she could share reminiscences with people who understood her attitudes and mistakes. Her friends had seemed to her a peaceful island in the midst of Calcutta's commotion. She had leaned heavily on their self-confidence.

Then after the first round of parties, the beliefs and omissions of her friends began to unsettle her. She was not an unpatriotic person, but she felt very distant from the passions that quickened or outraged her class in Calcutta. Her friends let slip their disapproval of her, they suggested her marriage had been imprudent, that the seven years abroad had eroded all that was fine and sensitive in her Bengali nature. They felt she deserved chores like washing her own dishes and putting out the garbage. The best that could be said for David, she sensed, was that he was, nominally at least, a Christian and not a Moslem.

Pronob's group irritated Tara with its lack of seriousness. The group often sat on the roof of the Catelli-Continental, imagining itself successful and splendid, smoking and swearing in public to flout conventions, imploring Tara not to smile at strange old men in blazers and sun hats. They longed to listen to stories about America, about television and automobiles and frozen foods and record players. But when she mentioned ghettos or student demonstrations her friends protested. What nonsense! They knew America was lovely, they knew New York was not like Calcutta.

Of course they preferred stories about the Calcutta they had all shared. They came back again and again to the nuns of St. Blaise's and to the Radio Ceylon disc jockeys they had worshiped as schoolchildren.

"Did you know Carefree Kevin wasn't English? He was Polish," said Nilima. She was a beautiful girl, a little too chubby perhaps, but a beautiful girl waiting to be married. Her parents were constantly interviewing relatives of possible bridegrooms. She entertained secret fantasies about movie stars like Uttam Kumar and Tony Perkins, and considered the efforts of her parents vulgar.

"My cousin in Bombay," began Tara, "saw Carefree Kevin once. She said he isn't too magnetic."

"What nonsense! Your cousin must be a liar."

One afternoon at the Catelli-Continental, which seemed to Tara much like all other afternoons at the café there, Pronob was unusually withdrawn and severe. Instead of answering their arguments with his own beliefs on disc jockeys and missionaries, he shouted, "Can you shut up for a sec, folks? I want to listen to the English news."

"Don't be a dashed bore," objected Nilima. "I don't want to hear about bombings. I want music instead."

Pronob, who was considered by the group to have a certain way with impetuous women, merely ignored Nilima and turned up the volume. "I have to find out if they intend to go through with the general strike," he said. "I'm telling you running a factory is turning me gray. They better not try any monkey tricks till Father gets back from Benares."

"This is All-India Radio Calcutta. Here is the news read by Gopal Kumar Bose."

It was hard for Tara to think of Pronob as a businessman. She remembered his long monologues, delivered with some passion, on Tagore and *Ravindra sangeet* when he had been a student. He had seemed to her sensitive then, he had seemed almost a poet. But he had become fat and ill-tempered in the past seven years. He had acquired an official title: Deputy Chairman of the Board of Directors, Flame Co., Ltd. He spent more and more time, in custom-made raw silk shirts and cottage industries ties, managing his father's match factory while his father, not yet sixty-two, spent more and more money purifying himself by the Ganges.

"There have been isolated skirmishes between the police and the demonstrators on Rashbehari Avenue near Deshaprya Park. Eight men have been taken to hospital."

"How dare they?" Pronob sounded horrified. "They are just trying to provoke the police into violence. How can they get away with it?"

"I'm afraid Pronob's awful once he gets started on these things. He loses all sense. He's no fun to be with," explained Reena.

Tara's first instinct was to tell her friends not to explain. She suspected she was in the presence of history, and their explanations, though well meant, would distract her. She was afraid she might miss the newscaster's words, might not know how many bombs had gone off where or how many people had been killed.

"I'm scared," Tara said. "Things sound awful."

"What nonsense you talk!" consoled Reena. "It's just a routine sort of thing. Actually, it used to be much worse before."

"Things were so bad that my mother wouldn't let me go to the movies, not even to the Metro," said Nilima.

"It's all a political stunt," said Pronob. "Farms are being looted, landlords are being clubbed to death. This is reform?"

An angry fat man, thought Tara, is pathetic. She was afraid of these moods in Pronob. They were hard to match with the moods of a young man who had once written poetry and a one-act play for children. She feared such passion would bring on a stroke or some worse tragedy. The other girls in Pronob's group paid no attention to his anger. They were busy recalling happier times when Carefree Kevin had taken charge of the Hit Parade, when Johnny Mathis had sung to them.

"Oh how lucky you are, Tara!" said the girls. "Tell us more about America. Tell us what you do every day."

There they were again, even Pronob, wanting to know what it was like being a Bengali girl in America, not how she had got there, nor why. She described to them in detail how she spent a typical day in New York, what she ate for breakfast, how much the subway token cost, how she washed and hung her nylons above the bathtub, what her thesis director looked like. Pronob wondered if the American quarter resembled the fifty-*naye-paise* coin, and if petrol was as expensive there as it was in Calcutta. He turned down the radio, so he could listen better to Tara.

"The marchers," said the newscaster softly, *"are proceeding in somewhat disorderly fashion. They have passed Firpo's and the Grand Hotel. The police have cordoned that area of the maidan . . ."*

"I wish Carefree Kevin could come back," sighed Nilima. "We all *loved* Carefree Kevin."

"It seems funny now," said Tara, "a Pole in Colombo turning on hundreds of impeccable St. Blaise's girls."

"Turning on?" asked Pronob.

"That's like, well, like making happy."

"Teach us more phrases, please. The words they are using right now in America."

"I would hate to be an immigrant," said Pronob suddenly. "I wouldn't mind giving up the factory, but I'd hate to be a nobody in America. How do they treat Indians, Tara?"

Tara started guiltily as if something she had hoped to hide had suddenly been forced out into the open. She envied the self-confidence of these people, their passionate conviction that they were always right. She could not imagine her friends as immigrants anywhere, much less looking for jobs and apartments in Chicago or Detroit. But, if the great-granddaughter of Hari Lal of Pachapara, the only daughter of the Bengal Tiger of Banerjee & Thomas [Tobacco] Co., Ltd. had adjusted to such loss, why could not Pronob and his gang?

"You don't have to be a nobody, you know," objected Tara. "I mean, someone like you with your experience in managing your own business could make a very comfortable living." She knew, of course, she had not convinced Pronob, that he thought such anonymity inadequate compensation for the loss of class power and privilege.

"*The first phalanx of the procession is nearing the Catelli-Continental Hotel.*"

"Look!" shouted Nilima. "Look down there! Those fellows are right under us now. Gosh! Aren't they awful? What if they come into the hotel and . . . and do something dreadful to us?"

The sight of the marchers filled Pronob with passionate cynicism. He saw them as the identifiable group behind *gheraos* of Flame Co., Ltd. "Calcutta's finished," he said. "These damn left-of-leftist politicians! They are going to force us to shoot it out with men like that. Calcutta will be a hell."

Nilima nestled closer to Pronob's raw-silk shoulders. She is being coy again, thought Tara, she is taking liberties under promise of danger, she is cultivating a look of helplessness.

"I say, there are women among them! What shameless exhibitionists!"

"I have an Aunt Binita," said Reena, "who took part in the More Milk for Mothers and Babies *gherao* at your uncle's office, Pronob. My mother was so embarrassed when she saw your cousin-sister at the Calcutta Club. But I think it's kind of cool to have a marching aunt." She turned to Tara for reassurance that her use of "cool" had been correct.

The procession jabbed its arms through the dusty air. From Tara's perch (she had climbed on a chair for a better view), at first the procession looked like a giant caterpillar, sluggish and quite harmless, on the busy road. Then she was able to make out banners, picket signs, bricks, soda bottles, bamboo poles. The leaders ran back and forth, coaxing people to shout louder and to get in the way of the traffic. It was strange, thought Tara, to see two cars, one a Morris Minor, the other a Fiat, bearing the only PRESS signs. There were no television cameras, no U.S. marshals. No one to manipulate or interpret the course of Calcutta's history. From the roof of the Catelli, Tara saw Calcutta, squeezed horribly together, men, women, infants, some scratching their crotches, others laughing like tourists in an unfamiliar section of town. And always the heartbeat of the slogans. "Blood bath! Blood bath! Blood bath! Blood bath!"

Tara shaded her eyes to see better. She felt safe on the roof, watching the slogan filter through the marchers, row by row, blending and changing, till the last ragged lines merely said, "Shed blood, blood shed, shed blood, blood shed." Customers darted out of expensive Chowringhee Avenue stores, carrying Swiss confectionery, handmade silks, sterling silver coffee sets, while the store owners tried to lock up their display cases.

"Your first demonstration, Tara. I hope you enjoy it."

Oh no, Tara thought. I saw Chicago on television, and Newark, and Detroit.

"Is that the leader? That chap wearing a red hanky on his head?"

"You mean Deepak Ghose? That bastard? This guy's too short. Ghose always looks so big in the newspaper pictures."

They waited for more, something more exciting, some little twist of violence on the streets. They felt closer than they had before, comforted by the threat below.

A marcher tried to hold up a taxi, and was pushed back into the procession by three policemen in red turbans. Tara was amazed to discover this small incident had genuinely frightened her.

"Why *three* policemen?" she asked the others. She hoped her fear would not force her into coy remarks and gestures like Nilima, who was now clinging to Pronob's hand with affectionate violence.

"*Heavy fighting has broken out in the Hindusthan Road area.*"

"Oh my God," said Tara, listening closely to the radio. "How will we get home, Pronob? I'm really scared."

"Life, my dear Tara, is too short for such seriousness. We are such stuff as dreams are made of and our little life rounded with a sleep."

"Don't worry," said Reena. "Pronob will see us all home. It isn't really as bad as it sounds on the radio. They are famous for exaggerating. Do you want a cigarette? Your folks won't find out if you chew a *pan* afterward."

On Chowringhee some marchers broke rank. But before going home they emptied garbage from the municipal dustbins. They walked into spacious stores. They overturned cars parked at the curb. And they slugged the doorkeeper of the Catelli-Continental Hotel.

10

THOUGH DAVID wrote regularly, the David of aerogrammes was unfamiliar to Tara. He seemed like a figure standing in shadows, or a foreigner with an accent on television.

> I miss you very much. But I understand you have to work this out. I just hope you get it over with quickly. How are your parents? Tell them they'll have to rustle up tiger hunts and moonlit Taj Mahals when I visit. The Mets are doing badly. I'm still reworking the fifth chapter of the novel, the part when Joseph goes to Sweden to meet Tonia. I think the next section is all right. Who is this businessman riding trains with you? I'm not sure I like it. Look after yourself. Remember the unseen dangers of India. Tell your parents to cable me if you get sick.

Tara could no longer visualize his face in its entirety, only bits and pieces in precise detail, and this terrified her. Each aerogramme caused her momentary panic, a sense of trust betrayed, of mistakes never admitted. It was hard to visualize him because she was in India, Tara thought. In India she felt she was not married to a person but to a foreigner, and this foreignness was a burden. It was hard for her to talk about marriage responsibilities in Camac Street; her friends were curious only about the adjustments she had made.

She sat in an uncomfortable chair in the hall, under a framed photograph of her great-grandfather, trying to compose a letter to her husband. It was hard to tell a foreigner that she loved him very much when she was surrounded by the Bengal Tiger's chairs, tables, flowers, and portraits. She made several beginnings, seizing the specific questions he had asked as anchors against her helplessness. Her parents, she said, were very well; of course, they worried about the bombings and recurring strikes, and the attitude of servants these days was not what it once had been, but they were both quite well. Mr. Tuntunwala, she said, was a famous and respectable person, extremely ugly and probably a bit vulgar, but she thought his implied hint about improper activities totally unnecessary and cruel. Her voice in these letters was insipid or shrill, and she tore them up, twinging at the waste of seventy-five *naye paise* for each mistake. She felt there was no way she could describe in an aerogramme the endless conversations at the Catelli-Continental, or the strange old man in a blazer who tried to catch her eye in the café, or the hatred of Aunt Jharna or the bitterness of slogans scrawled on walls of stores and hotels.

It was hard, after the welcome from her parents, after the teas and celebrations of her St. Blaise's friends, to think of the 120th Street apartment as home. She remembered how the first semester at Vassar she had clung to the large leather suitcase bought for her in a hurry by the Bengal Tiger at New Market, how she had refused to unpack.

Tara idly scratched grease from the photograph above her head, and discovered Hari Lal's toes locked in a yogic position. She knew from stories she must have heard her mother tell that in that photograph Hari Lal sat fiercely Brahminical and shirtless, that he had maintained his yogic posture long after the photographer had gone away. *I am sitting under my great-*

grandfather's picture, she began again. But that too had to be discarded. David was hostile to genealogies and had often misunderstood her affection for the family as overdependence.

Her mother entered the hall, looking extremely agitated. "Taramoni, haven't you finished yet?"

"I just got started."

"Then the letter must wait for tomorrow. I can't tell you what is going on. *Hai hai!*"

Tara was surprised by her mother's emotion. Her mother was not given to melodrama, only to theories about Moslems. She explained she intended to take her time over the letter, then drive to the post office and pay a late fee so it would go out that night.

"What is this nonsense! The *durwan* says there is too much fighting everywhere."

"No! Again?"

"Not like before. He says a three-year-old girl was killed."

"Where's Daddy?"

"I can tell you he won't let you go. We can send the *durwan* with your letter. *Hai hai!* Never did I think Bengalis would kill like Moslems!"

Tara declined the offer to send the *durwan* to the post office. She expressed fears the *durwan* would be caught by rioters. But her mother laughed at her naiveté and explained that rioters were not after *durwans,* only after the upper classes. She forbade Tara to worry. Her father would find a way of sending the letter to the post office in spite of street violence. In any case Tara should include her parents' "heartfelt and most joyous blessings" to David and "sincere greetings" to David's mother.

Tara put away her pen and aerogrammes. She wished she had not come to India without her husband.

11

SANJAY BASU, assistant editor of the *Calcutta Observer,* thought of himself as a wild bachelor. His days were dedicated to the pursuit of Truth, his evenings to the pursuit of Beauty. Goodness did not enter into his calculations. On Mondays he attended the weekly British Council debate. On Tuesdays he went to Anuradha's jazz soiree. On Wednesday nights he went to the movies; on Thursday nights to the Literary Circle on Lake Temple Road, Fridays and Saturdays to parties, and Sundays to his ancestral home in Barrackpore to visit his grandmother.

This Monday evening Sanjay was a little more agitated than usual. He was to speak to the British Council debate. The motion on the floor was: *English should be abolished as an official language in India.* Sanjay would speak against the motion. He had worked for days to acquire a desired supercilious tone and gesture.

Sanjay's little Fiat with the PRESS signs on the front and back windows darted around buses, cars, taxis, scooters, lorries, bullock carts, occasional cows and pedestrians on Chittaranjan Avenue, emerged on the wider and still more crowded Chowringhee, turned left on Park Street, made a frivolous right into Havelock Row to look at the classy St. Blaise's girls, and finally turned into Camac Street.

He loved Camac Street. He was writing an article on it for a foreign newspaper.

When the heart reaches Camac Street it discovers the old Calcutta, the fair Calcutta, the Calcutta that never again will be. It has no quarrel with the English for it is too rich and too sophisticated to be peevish. There are few houses on Camac Street and those that are there are set far back from the sidewalks. The houses are immense and they mystify the poorer Calcations and enrage the nouveau riche. These houses are not houses but veritable compounds. Within the walled compounds are aging gardeners, beautiful women, spoiled dogs, and liveried servants.

Sanjay was pleased with the opening paragraph of his article. It captured his love of Camac Street. He felt warm and safe there. Parents of his friends occupied five homes on this street, though the friends themselves had moved out to New Alipore. He did not like New Alipore; it was brash and showy; it lacked the mystery and calm of Camac Street, he often said.

The British Council occupied a large house with wrought iron window grilles and spacious enclosed verandahs on Theatre Road, off Camac Street. Its gardens were well maintained and its gatekeeper *salaamed* Sanjay as he stepped out of his tiny car. It pleased Sanjay immensely to be greeted by wardens of such public places. He managed a smile in return in spite of his nervousness.

He was greeted at the main door by Mr. Worthington, a pale Londoner with a slight trace of dandruff. Mr. Worthington prided himself in being one of a new breed of British Council directors and sought opportunities to inform the Indians that he had gone to Essex rather than Oxford or Cambridge. He was essentially a kind, if rather innocent young man, who liked to wear Indian dress on Sundays and eat curry with his fingers.

Looking spry in a blue Italian shirt and striped pants, Sanjay cut through the crowd to a knot of British Council regulars. He showered compliments on Miss Dutta, the lone female speaker, who had a reputation for being learned and therefore was not expected to be pretty. The audience, large and docile, elated him. He thought he detected admiring glances from college girls and he responded by looking handsome and confident. In the far left corner of the room he spotted Pronob and his group and nodded slightly to them as he rehearsed his speech. He noted Pronob had brought a stranger. And because he considered himself the custodian of Calcutta's records, he knew the strange girl's name, that her father was the redoubtable Dr. "Bengal Tiger" Banerjee of Banerjee & Thomas [Tobacco] Co., Ltd., and that she had gone to Idaho or Ohio or someplace to study. But there was no time to speculate on the girl's presence nor to wonder if she would discover mistakes in his grammar. Mr. Worthington was coughing to get his attention. Mr. Worthington's fiancée (Sanjay knew Worthington slept with her on weekends and he enjoyed his own tolerance of such lasciviousness) was playing a few bars from the popular song "Oh, Why Can't the English Learn to Speak?" on an old piano. The audience was appreciative of her talent and choice, and amid this knowing hilarity the debate commenced.

"Ladies and gentlemen, charming ladies and witty gentlemen," began the Englishman, leaning awkwardly across a low table where he had placed a pitcher of iced water, a bell and an alarm clock. "Perhaps by the end of the evening, if the motion wins, I shall be saying *Bhai ebong bon* or *bhaio boheno* . . ."

The audience did not recognize the actual Bengali or Hindi phrase cowering under the young man's thick London accent, but they recognized the goodness of his intentions and clapped madly.

When it was Sanjay's turn to speak superciliousness deserted him. He told the people that Calcutta was in danger, that he was an assistant editor of a reputable newspaper, that he was exposed more than others to the horrors of the city's changes. He begged everyone to remember their traditions, their conscience, their English if they wished to save themselves from lawless ruin. With passion and intensity he urged them to hold on to a Calcutta that was disappearing like mist.

Miss Dutta, however, sprang to her feet. Calcutta cannot disappear like mist, she scorned, for Calcutta has never had any mists. Mists for Bengalis were linguistic tricks; like buttercups and nightingales, in Calcutta they simply did not exist. And poor Sanjay forgot the words and wit he had intended to exercise. He sought refuge in poetry instead, quoting erratically from Tennyson and Keats and Sassoon to prove points he had abused or missed altogether.

After it was all over and the audience had disappeared down the staircase into the library rooms below, and the select few had stayed back for sherry and biscuits in Worthington's private quarters, Pronob introduced Sanjay to Tara. For Sanjay it was an uncomfortable meeting. He still suffered from the disgrace inflicted by Miss Dutta. Though he talked to Tara of the weather, made much of his brief trip to Boston in 1960 when he had lost his Sholapuri sandals in a tourist room on Brattle Street, he was sure the girl was laughing at him. With Reena he knew he could be witty, with Nilima devastating; but with Tara who knew nothing of his journalistic, poetic and amorous coups, he was utterly lost. He stood there, handsome and helpless in his imported shirt and bell-bottom pants, while Tara asked him silly questions about a protest march he had recently covered.

"Did a three-year-old kid really die?"

"Oh yes. What do you think? We journalists are reliable."

"These demonstrators . . ."

"They're hoodlums! They're *goondahs* trying to crack the Establishment. But they get their heads cracked instead." Sanjay repeated the phrase. He liked the balanced quibbling with the word "crack" and filed it away for use in a future British Council debate. "My best phrases come to me when I'm talking to girls!"

Tara did not seem to hear his compliment. She was too full of

questions about the conduct of the police, the tactics of the rioters, editorials he had written.

"Have they ever tried to burn your car?"

"You're kidding!" Sanjay exploded. "Don't you know who's
the inspector in charge of these shows?"

"No."

"It's old P.S. We play tennis every Saturday at the South Tri-
angle Club."

Tara told him how much easier she thought it was to live in
Calcutta. How much simpler to trust the city's police inspector
and play tennis with him on Saturdays. How humane to accompany a friendly editor to watch the riots in town. New York, she
confided, was a gruesome nightmare. It wasn't muggings she
feared so much as rude little invasions. The thought of a stranger, a bum from Central Park, a Harlem dandy, looking into her
pocketbook, laughing at the notes she had made to herself, observations about her life and times, old sales slips accumulated
over months for merchandise long lost or broken, credit cards,
identification cards with unflattering pictures by which a criminal could identify her. And more than the muggings the waiting to be mugged, fearing the dark that transformed shoddy
innocuous side streets into giant fangs crouching, springing to
demolish this one last reminder of the Banerjees of Pachapara.

Sanjay was embarrassed by this outburst. Behind Tara, the
select few were singing "For He's a Jolly Good Fellow" to
Worthington, who smiled back like a man who is content to be
decent, intelligent and popular. He was anxious to join in the
singing tribute to Worthington.

"I'll keep in touch," Sanjay said as he fled from Tara.

12

AT NIGHT on Park Street, in a six-room flat leased for him by the company, Joyonto thought of the young woman he had pledged to protect one rash afternoon at the Catelli-Continental. The flat, though luxurious and old-fashioned, was stuffed with an astonishing mixture of Moghul swords, Sankhera chairs, Victorian mirrors, Jacobean sofas and Chinese Buddhas. Joyonto was aware of the failure of his taste in decorating his home. But he prided himself in that failure. It was the failure of a vanished Calcutta, of a decade when men carrying ladders had stopped by his house to light gas lamps at nightfall, when there had been few trams and cars to burn. He had loved Calcutta then, its gargoyled houses, its business districts where some men tried valiantly to wear bowler hats, even its courts where justice, he suspected, was not always done. But now, by the window, watching the electric light skim the tops of flower baskets, Joyonto thought again of the sober young woman in the café and his desire to protect her.

It would have been a relief if he had been like other old men, intact though weary. He could have retired and gone on a world cruise, taken up gardening or bird watching or some other hobby. But Joyonto, the owner of foothills in Assam and estates in Tollygunge, felt trapped by his assets. He had had to know too many people, remember too many details, see too many things. Yes, that was it, he had seen too much from his perch at the Catelli. He had witnessed men club each other and he had been moved by their violence.

Joyonto walked to the liquor cabinet in the library, where the walls were soft with street lighting. Glasses, rare and unmatched, were neatly laid out on a silver tray. He had picked up the cabinet and the glasses at an auction just after the fierce communal riots of 1947. That was all the riots were to him, a unique chance for bargain antiques. He had collected Czechoslovakian finger bowls from terrified survivors and not once had he admitted any regret. There was no color, not even from dust, in his glass (his widowed aunt who supervised the servants had seen to that), and the ice cubes were clear though bacteria-ridden, the gin clear and syrupy.

On the far wall a flat sword, too decorative to be efficient, teased him with memories of his mother, whom Joyonto always referred to as "a first-class lady." His mother had given him the sword and told him it once belonged to the Rani of Jhansi. With that sword, his mother liked to say, the Rani had driven Robert Clive, "a delinquent hoodlum," out of her palace. In his mother's stories the Indians always won and their world, ritualistic, aristocratic, always remained secure. Joyonto did not consider himself a winner like his mother or the Rani of Jhansi. He was more like the legendary *nawab* who almost lost his life to the invading British because his valet had fled and there was none left to help him tie his shoelaces.

At school in history class the missionaries had made Robert Clive a hero so brave that he had conquered India *and* put a stop to the odious practice of burning Bengali widows. But I like *sati,* his mother the "first-class lady" always protested. If I survive your father, please burn me on his pyre, I don't want to live without him. She had indeed burned with him, fastened to her seat by a protective belt, burned on the foothills of the Himalayas, the holy mountains, watched by the gods as their tiny Dakota crashed among the evergreens a few miles from their tea estates.

Joyonto was troubled by these memories though he had called them up often, had polished and honed them as if they were prized instruments. He was sure his mother returned to this room, hid herself beneath a Victorian mirror or Chinese Buddha and judged him every day.

If she were still alive, he thought, she would not be crushed by the city's changes. He was sure of that, just as he was sure he himself would always respond wrongly. In earlier crises when his mother had worn handloom saris, when handloom had meant defiance, stirrings of the heart in Christian boarding schools and homemade bombs in gym lockers, Joyonto had quietly suffered the knighting of a great-uncle at Buckingham Palace.

The night was darker now, some neon signs had been switched off, and only the destitute in shapeless huddles remained on Park Street. Rats and roaches slithered from the moisture, gnawed on tattered saris, possessed the streets and alleys. Joyonto was afraid. His hands scurried over his naked torso, his fingers as light as spiders' legs, leaving damp nervous patches on his ribs and spine. He felt that his mother and the city had judged and left him condemned.

Beneath his window refugees and professional beggars grunted in their sleep. Joyonto saw a woman directly below him, ungainly mother of indeterminate age, legs locked together, one nipple exposed where an infant had tugged it. At the Catelli-Continental these destitutes were made acceptable by the hotel's livery. As waiters they brought him sandwiches, tea, and coffee. Their faces bore no rage, no hatred as they served ruminating gentlemen like him. But here in Park Street he sometimes felt he recognized their faces, he thought he saw them urinating in public.

Now he could only wait for some final catastrophe to break over him. He would not listen to his mother, whose presence still curled about the room. He would wait and submit instead.

He would wait for the first gray streaks of a false dawn to dim the streetlights of Park Street. The waiting of course wearied him. Finally he admitted it had been a bad night, full of anti-climactic premonitions. No vision or revelation would come to him. In despair he flexed his legs, leaped on the Kashmiri rug in the center of the room, and threw himself into the simplest yoga exercises his body could still command.

But just before the false dawn while Joyonto was standing on his head, eyes popping behind closed lids with unaccustomed strain, the vision he awaited snickered at him through the window grilles, stretched its shadow over the house and all the city. Sleeping bodies stirred as the rodents of the night found their daytime cover. Night had passed and the vision shriveled. It nestled in a million corners, in cups and drawers and folds of saris. Joyonto retired. They found him at noon, drunk in the sixth room as usual, when the servants, led by the widowed aunt, were purifying all the rooms in accordance with holy ritual.

13

THERE WERE CHAINS of multicolored electric lights in the garden of the Ramraj Palace, which since 1952 had become the property of the Asian Tractor Company. The Calcutta Chamber of Commerce had selected the palace grounds for its annual charity carnival. The gates of the palace were decorated with young banana trees in clay pots, and festooned by mango leaves. Urchins stood in large numbers outside the main gates. They gaped at the revelers who arrived by the carful, asked for *baksheesh*, and were turned away. Within the walled palace, rows of attractive food stalls, souvenir boutiques and entertainment platforms had been erected by the prominent legations, consulates, manufacturers, airline companies, the Rotary Club and the Lions Club.

Tara, standing between Sanjay and Pronob, who were sampling Swiss cheeses, spied a small, compact man at the other end of the stall. She recognized him as the National Personage she had met in the train on her way from Bombay to Calcutta, and she slipped out from the center of Pronob's Group, so that she might be seen.

"So we meet again," said P. K. Tuntunwala, and folded his hands in a *namaste*.

If it were not for the fact that she had met Tuntunwala on the train and had been drawn strangely to him, Tara thought, she would have found him a repulsively ugly man.

"How do you like Calcutta now?" the National Personage asked.

"It hasn't changed much," she heard herself answer with a girlish laugh. "They had these carnival things when I was a schoolgirl."

He did not believe her, though she struggled to convince him that all her childhood friends were the same as before, that the old movie houses were still there, the old nightclubs, even the nuns who had taught her. He responded with hostility, and she liked him because he did not believe her.

"I cannot tell you what a weritable hell is Calcutta."

He talked bitterly of licenses, import restrictions, pension plans for workers, shortage of investment capital, *gheraos* as Tara followed from stall to stall. They walked through the noisy, magical darkness of the charity carnival, picking at cold pizzas. She was reminded again of a spider, small, ugly, teasing a Nepali in a railway compartment somewhere between Bombay and Calcutta. They paused briefly at the American pavilion as a tribute to David and bought two hot dogs.

"I am a very modern man," said P. K. Tuntunwala. "I have learned to eat pork."

Tara found the National Personage a fast walker. It was hard for her to keep up with him as he moved from counter to counter, making small purchases. He always checked the clerks' additions, occasionally pointed out a mistake, and left the managers of stalls in ill humor. Soon she began to anticipate his pattern. First the salesgirl's eagerness, then Tuntunwala's request for some trivial merchandise or souvenir, next his dissatisfaction with the stock offered, his request for more merchandise, his small and reluctant purchase, followed by his checking and rechecking of the bill, and finally his calculation of the change to be returned.

"What a lot of nonsense this is! Come, I will show you something ten *lakh* times better," said P. K. Tuntunwala finally.

They hurried past women with baggy midriffs throwing Ping-Pong balls into buckets and beautiful girls from St. Blaise's smoking behind trees. Now and then Tuntunwala was stopped by fat Marwaris in beige suits, carrying plush teddy bears and other small trophies. Tara thought Mr. Tuntunwala treated these men with disdain. She wondered at herself for following him, he was so different from the men she knew or admired, so different from her father for instance. She was sure he did not share her Bengali attitudes, that he was not a businessman like Pronob. He showed too much energy.

As they walked a woman who had held a tea for Tara ran up to them with giggling opinions on a new American Western showing at The Old Paradise Cinema. But the Marwari with the deplorable manners led Tara away before she could confess she had not seen the movie.

"I cannot tell you how upset movies make me. They are unreal and silly. A weritable waste of time," Mr. Tuntunwala said with feeling.

They strolled past a small circular platform where four young men with greasy hair crooned English songs from the fifties into a difficult mike. Past blonde old women in shiny jockeys' outfits standing before the booth of the Tollygunge Turf Association. Past an earnest white man in shirt-sleeves demonstrating typewriters and adding machines. Then finally they saw it; they saw Tuntunwala's carnival exhibit.

It was set apart from everything else in the Ramraj Palace by bamboo barriers and canvas hangings. Strung between two mango trees was a neon sign: THE TUNTUNCO MILLS BOOTIK STALL. The walls and ceiling were hung with mirrors that reflected cascades of cotton thread, textiles, towels, sheets, pillowcases, bedspreads, dusters and saris. Here and there, peeking through loops of merchandise, were thirty young Charulata Home Science College girls, well-bred and almost pretty, masquerading for the evening as nymphs, driads and Hindu angels. It was by far the largest stall on the grounds.

Tara was moved by the Marwari's desire to show her his stall. "It's splendid," she remarked.

Tuntunwala stood silent and worshipful before the display. "Oh come, come. It is a very very small operation," he said with the air of a man who rules kingdoms rather than businesses.

He walked briskly up the shallow steps that led to his stall. Tara saw him surrounded by Tuntunco Mills products. He raised both arms while cunning lights played on his little black face and on his white sharkskin suit. He gave a signal, and the thirty Charulata Home Science College girls left their positions amid drip-dry sheets and soft dusting cloths to group themselves around him. A Tuntunco Mills public-relations officer readied his flash bulb to immortalize the scene.

Though Tara was not given to intuitions, she thought the Marwari's ease and mastery frightening. In the new and powerful light she noted a scar under the man's left eye, a sign perhaps of some difficult victory. She knew he was incapable of defeat.

Then he motioned to Tara to join him for the picture, and though she did not like the peremptoriness of his gestures, she knew she would obey without much questioning. Tuntunwala settled her in an armchair upholstered with Tuntunco Mills fabric, then struck a declaratory pose. He addressed her energetically, attacking communists in Calcutta, general strikes, looting of private homes, predicting murders of rival leaders and "weritable godlessness or ten *lakh* times more worse things."

"I must move to Bombay!" he concluded with a flourish. "Yes, I have decided. Calcutta is too damned for all this!" He waved his frail arms to take in the stall and the thirty virginal models.

A nymph draped in printed voile brought Tara a fresh lemon and soda drink. Appalled by the fervor of the Marwari's speech, she tried to make jokes of his predictions.

"You must be putting me on," she said as a St. Blaise's girl on the other side of the bamboo barrier waved to her in envy.

"I'm very definitely not putting anyone anywhere," said Mr. Tuntunwala. The *goondahs* and other such evil elements are doing all the putting, I tell you."

It was an unseemly moment, thought Tara, for an apocalypse. She could see a heavy woman in a chiffon sari throw rings at plastic ducks. A tightly vested man stumbled and broke six jars of lemon pickle that he had been hugging. A family of eight stood in a circle eating Chinese food from cartons.

"You are teasing me," she insisted, nervously jingling a pearl and ruby bangle that her unfortunate Great-Aunt Arupa had worn at her wedding long ago. Mr. Tuntunwala was a dangerous man. He could create whatever situation, whatever catastrophe he needed. It was no use criticizing him, Tara thought; the only thing to do was to get out of his stall. She felt badly now that she had deserted Pronob and Sanjay. They were her kind of Bengali. They could be trusted to enjoy her jokes and attitudes. And they were charming, even witty. "Excuse me. I've got to join my friends now. They'll be worrying about me."

"Nothing to worry!" exclaimed the National Personage. "We haven't as yet begun our fun. Come, come, we too must throw quoits at ducks like that lovely lady there."

And Tara, looking around in panic at the thirty models for some sign of pity, was given three plastic rings. Outside the gates of the Ramraj Palace the urchins tired, fell asleep or dead, and were replaced by other urchins till they too fell asleep.

14

THE MAY MORNING was unusually dry. On Chowringhee the puddles left by street cleaners were shriveling in the gutters, and the beggars were hanging out their rags to dry on the municipal trees. At the Catelli-Continental the waiters shook out their limp uniforms, set up brightly colored tables and chairs and umbrellas, and opened for business as usual. At one time not long ago a dry sunny day would have brought out thirty or forty mothers, daughters and aging observers to the umbrellas of the Catelli-Continental. But now the almost daily riots frightened away most customers.

Tara came once a week without her friends so she could read at the Catelli-Continental. In the hotel lobby she could buy foreign newspapers and magazines. She always bought the *Times* of London, and old issues of *The New Yorker* and the *Herald-Tribune*. But these weekly rituals left her more confused than ever. She read of crises in foreign stock markets, ads for villas in

Spain, presidential commissions, the Mets, hoping the foreign news would bring her closer to David.

This May morning she worked carefully through "Goings On About Town" in *The New Yorker*. She read of Mormon Art exhibits on Madison Avenue and of sculpture by Archipenko during his Paris period. She had never heard of Archipenko, perhaps no one else in Calcutta had either. She had visions of David taking girls to see Archipenko's work, girls who knew about such things and were committed to Women's Liberation, girls like Susie Goldberg.

Then there was a voice by her shoulder, and an old man in a blazer was smiling at her just as he had smiled at her from a far table for many weeks now at the Catelli-Continental.

"I'm Joyonto Roy Chowdhury, fast friend of your daddy."

Tara thought him an odd little man with a gnome's face, and she recalled Pronob's warnings against talking to strangers in Calcutta. But he had already ordered the waiter to bring his tea and toast to her table.

"Your name is Mrs. Cartwright, no? I've seen your picture in the *Feminine Weekly*."

She looked at him coldly; it bothered her that a strange old man had seen her picture, had perhaps taken the magazine to his room so he could study the smudged details of her face. Mr. Roy Chowdhury pushed his tea aside and began involved and pointless stories about his childhood in Pachapara. Tara kept her eyes on the *Times*; other people's memories had always fatigued her. There were comforting sounds around her, shrill giggles from other tables, cups clanking on waiters' trays, and beyond that traffic noises from Chowringhee Avenue. Some phrases came to her, strange words and combinations that she quickly assumed she had imagined, not heard. *Smoky tea, luminous child, poor scratched crow*, she thought she heard such words and was reassured when the old man suggested they take "a breath of fresh air."

Fresh air of course was impossible in Calcutta; she thought it typical of the old man to invent so simple an excuse to take her out. Perhaps his stories had really been hypnotic or perhaps she had been thinking of David, who accused her of having become utterly passive. She found herself agreeing that it was a gorgeous day for a ride and that she would be delighted to accompany him briefly as long as they drove in *her* car. Old men are stubborn. Mr. Roy Chowdhury insisted they take his car, that he was likely to get sick and would be embarrassed if that happened in hers. Tara was surprised at the quickness of her own decision to accompany a stranger. In Calcutta proprieties were paralyzing. While the old man fretted about cars and chauffeurs, she sensed the start of a small adventure. She thought an adventure would come in handy when she wrote David her biweekly letter. David was growing impatient. He had almost said that he thought her lazy, not doing enough, that inertia was the Indian's curse. In the end they traveled in Mr. Roy Chowdhury's '57 Dodge, followed by Tara's petulant chauffeur in her Rover.

Mr. Roy Chowdhury and Tara were driven south through alleys that curled around tenement slums and sudden parks. They passed the Kali temple in Kalighat, where Tara would have liked to stop. But the old man complained that shrines were always dark and stuffy and ordered his man to drive on. Only when they were by the river did Tara realize the old man's goal. He wanted to show her the funeral pyres.

It was a quiet hour on the funerary banks. Just one corpse was burning, and that too at such a distance that it seemed to occur in a faded snapshot. There were no priests nearby, no bereaved relatives, none of the tightly wired bouquets from

Hindu weddings and funerals. Only an upturned string bed which had carried a poor man's dead body, and some garden flowers. Tara thought it was not really frightening, this first look at the banks where death was proper. There were no sounds except a *Hari bol* chant from the burning pyre and the muddy slap of the river against the cement steps of the *ghat*.

Joyonto Roy Chowdhury proposed a walk along the bank as if he were suggesting a constitutional, and she agreed that it was a splendid idea. Pronob might have been right as far as it went — one shouldn't speak to strangers; saying yes to anyone in Calcutta was madness. But the banks were so silent and gentle. The city seemed to have faded on the far shore of the river. The cunning world of slums and beggars, of sunless alleys and barricaded storefronts had disappeared. The only sound as they got out was of the river washing the *ghat* and Tara's chauffeur polishing the car.

Then suddenly they heard a song with many trills. A tall thin man in scarlet loincloth jumped from his hiding place behind Joyonto's Dodge. Tara recognized him as a *tantric* from his dress and matted hair. Her first knowledge of *tantrics* had come to her through a Bombay cousin, who had described them as ghouls living among funeral pyres. Only much later had she learned that the Bombay cousin had lied, that *tantrics* were instead religious men.

The singing *tantric* held out his hand to Tara. She hoped he wanted *baksheesh* and quickly gave him two rupees. But the wild man laughed and flung the money at Joyonto's chauffeur. "Your palm."

Tara ran. She ran and stopped and ran again, not used to this kind of fear, dodged between the two cars that stood like carcasses, and stopped by the hood of the Rover so the *tantric* would not see her. Then she fumbled in her purse for a likely weapon, some forgotten penknife perhaps or pretty stone, and finding none — her purse was empty of complications in Calcutta — she stretched her neck around the corner, saw first the silvery grid of the car, then a curious tableau: the wild man reading Joyonto's palm. She waited a moment longer, and thinking it safe, dashed into the Rover and banged the door shut.

That noise was her triumph. It was shoddy and mean, she knew, but a triumph nevertheless. Her chauffeur stood ready, awaiting her order. Beyond the shadow of the Dodge the wild man pressed Joyonto's fingers and pointed to what she imagined were lines and stars on the mounds of his palm. Then the *tantric* walked away, baring long black teeth at the old man in blazer. To Tara it looked like a smile.

"*If I should die*," recited Mr. Roy Chowdhury as he came toward her, "*think only this of me: that there's some corner of a foreign field that is forever . . .*"

So madness was as simple as that, a wild man in loincloth reading palms and an old man in sandals reciting Rupert Brooke. Now her faith in Joyonto Roy Chowdhury was slowly breaking. She had hoped he could guide her through the new Calcutta, but his face seemed sinister as it pushed in through the open window of the Rover. He did not finish the sonnet. He stuck his hand in through the rectangle, unlocked the door and sat in the car beside her. There were little gray spots on his face. He had begun to slump, his breath was shallow and noisy, and with each gasp the loose skin around his neck shivered. Tara thought he was going to be sick. She had always disliked people with minor imperfections, people who fell asleep at public lectures or coughed at the movies. Joyonto had no business to be ill at the funeral pyres. She leaned toward him, planting both elbows on the armrest that divided the back seat. The old man looked much worse. Tara thought that paisley ascots were absurd on a dying savior, that his sandals, his blazer, his hair, all were unsuited to the occasion. She hoped it would be easy to leave him. He was after all a stranger.

"Do something," Tara snapped at Joyonto's chauffeur. "What's the matter with your *sahib?* He's dying or something!"

The chauffeur quickly assumed control, telling her not to worry, that his master was given to spells, that she should return home at once. Then he seized the limp body under the arms and carried it to the Dodge.

She had acted foolishly, she knew that of course. She had not listened to the cautions of her friends and she had abandoned a sick old man by the funeral pyres. She wondered if Joyonto Roy Chowdhury would be all right in the hands of his servant. Or would she, sitting with Pronob and his group over iced coffees at the Catelli, read of his death in a paragraph, and would a corner of Calcutta die with the old man in a blazer?

15

SOMETIMES for a change of pace Tara and her friends went to Kapoor's Restaurant. Kapoor's was not just a café, there are many smaller and smarter cafés on Park Street; it was (Sanjay often said) the symbol of modern India. The opening of this restaurant had been blessed by two cabinet ministers, one Brahmin priest, the cutting of several ribbons and an editorial by Sanjay in the *Calcutta Observer*. Its opening had marked the end of tea shops like Arioli's and Chandler's, where straw-hatted European ladies discussed the natives and the beastly weather over tea and cakes and mutton patties in shaded rooms cooled by *punkhas*. Kapoor's was long, dark and narrow, sealed off from the street by heavy doors. Its interior, unevenly air-conditioned, was crowded with bright and young Indians who talked in fractured vernaculars. At Kapoor's there was no need to imitate the West or to applaud the songs of shapely Anglo-Indian crooners. No need for Indian men and women to hold each other stiffly and coax the body into foreign dancing postures. *It is a relief,* Sanjay had written in his editorial, *to come to Kapoor's to sit and eat and talk, for there is nothing hostile here in the wallpapers. There are only deep vinyl seats, Formica tables, plants and narcissistic mirrors. Kapoor's Restaurant has calculated the longings of modern India.*

Since Tara's trip to the funeral *ghats* a terrible depression had overcome her. Her friends wanted to help. At first they tried to distract her with movies and concerts and *pakoras* at Kapoor's. But when that proved useless they called her "a silly billy" and "a bloody bore" and scolded her. They diagnosed her melancholy as "love sickness," and offered to cable David to join her in Calcutta. For nice Bengalis, thought Tara, to be depressed was to be stupid. Their sanity depended on their being lighthearted and casual in difficult situations. If allowed to develop, this silly-billiness could soil one's carefully bathed body, could result in pimples on the chin. Even Tara's Great-Aunt Arupa had known the dangers of this mood. Had she not gone mad from despair?

Standing outside Kapoor's one afternoon in early June she thought it best to return to New York. She had seen three children eat rice and yoghurt off the sidewalk. And this not in some furtive alley or slum, but on Park Street, where girls like Tara walked. Her friends told her the children were hardy, that they were used to such life, that they were not like "us people." And more painful than the words of her friends had been the joy on the faces of the children as they devoured their rice and yoghurt.

She wished she could talk to Joyonto Roy Chowdhury, but he had disappeared from the Catelli and the waiters would not disclose his whereabouts.

Sanjay hinted there was something vaguely unpatriotic about her depression. He ordered a plate of cheese *pakoras* and suggested she had surely been depressed in New York too. It was outrageous, he believed, to blame it all on Calcutta. The others ordered the "Superdeliteful Snakes" from the menu, and ignored Tara's moods.

"I'd like a cold coffee."

"I want an American Pride and *samosas*."

"What's that?"

"It's a tall, fuzzy drink. Pink at the bottom."

"Fizzy?" asked Tara.

Their snubs brought out minor viciousness in Tara. She insisted on correcting the grammatical errors of her friends, made jokes about their mannerisms, then waited to be shunned. But the group did not desert her. They decided Tara's depression was really boredom and boredom was the affliction of their class. They made new and heroic efforts to humor her. They wrote long letters to David, who wrote back to Tara that the letters were priceless. They planned a picnic at the Botanical Gardens and canceled it only when the Bengal Tiger insisted that the gardens were no longer safe from *goondahs*. They talked of moonlit drives and fancy dress balls and finally settled for a picnic on the factory premises of Banerjee & Thomas [Tobacco] Co., Ltd.

The group was charmed by its decision. It felt it finally had a focus. It met several times at Kapoor's to decide about the date for the picnic. Sanjay and Pronob were busy men after all, they couldn't go dashing off without canceling appointments or rescheduling others. The girls scribbled names of guests and telephone numbers on paper napkins at the restaurant.

"What about Suniti?"

"What nonsense! She didn't invite us to hers!"

"What about Roma Sen?"

"What nonsense! She married her weird Nigerian and went off at least a month ago."

"How dare you say that. She was such a nice girl, no?"

The friends expressed their disapproval of Roma Sen's marriage, then continued with the guest list. They were racial purists, thought Tara desperately. They liked foreigners in movie magazines — Nat Wood and Bob Wagner in faded *Photoplays*. They loved Englishmen like Worthington at the British Council. But they did not approve of foreign marriage partners. So much for the glamour of her own marriage. She had expected admiration from these friends. She had wanted them to consider her marriage an emancipated gesture. But emancipation was suspicious — it presupposed bondage. In New York she had often praised herself, especially when it was time to clean the toilet or bathtub. She had watched the bubbly blue action of the toilet cleanser, and had confided to David that at home there was a woman just to clean bathrooms. There was no heroism for her in New York. It appeared there would be no romance, no admiration in Calcutta either. It had been foolish, she knew, to expect admiration. The years away from India had made her self-centered. She took everything, the heat, the beggars, as personal insults and challenges. That explained her pained response to the children too, but the others had remained calm. She would try to imitate the others. She feared she might break down and cry in Kapoor's Restaurant.

"I'd like an iced coffee, please," said Tara to the waiter.

16

DURING THE WEEK of preparations for the picnic Tara felt very close to her father. Though he remained pot-bellied and authoritarian all day battling business competitors, he seemed to reserve his best energy for the evenings when he sat with his family in the verandah and planned the details of the guest list. On those evenings Tara thought she could see in her father the young man he once must have been. At twenty, she knew, the Bengal Tiger had published a short story about a Brahmin boy in love. And just before the Second World War, when he had been "recently foreign-returned," German girls had sent him picture post cards with illegible inscriptions. Talking about the picnic seemed to return to him the romance of those younger years.

"This is like the olden times, no?" the Bengal Tiger often said as he sat on the brocaded swing and looked at his daughter. "All these years we're feeling lonely without you. Now we'll have fun!"

From the start, however, the picnic at the guest house was destined to be a failure. For instance, it was discovered just as the cars were about to leave for the picnic that there was not enough room for all the guests, servants, mattresses, sheets and bolsters. At least three servants had to crouch in the luggage area of an old station wagon, which meant that their best holiday turbans were badly crushed. Pronob complained bitterly about the smallness of Indian cars and wished India had raised a company like General Motors.

Barrackpore Trunk Road goes right past the main gates of Banerjee & Thomas [Tobacco] Co., Ltd. It is a commercial artery, clogged with bicycles, automobiles, lorries, buses, bullock carts, pushcarts, motor scooters and pedestrians. It offers the Bengali traveler a delightful opportunity for chauvinism as it winds past warehouses, factories and other impressive landmarks. Sanjay and Pronob wittily pointed out the industrial charms of the landscape to Tara, but she was too distracted by the pushcarts to listen to them. Once she counted two children and twenty enormous sacks of potatoes on a single cart, a single frail man jogging with it down the highway.

"I simply love B.T. Road," cried Nilima as the car Pronob's group was in avoided one pothole after another. "It gives me a tremendous sense of freedom!" She liked to think of herself as a passionate girl. Her passion increased with each dangerous semicircle described by the chauffeur as he overtook lorries driven by hairy Sikhs, bell-less bicycles, and slow Hindustan Motors ambassadors. Then the car ran over broken glass and ground to a halt with a flat tire.

The entire convoy stopped. The older picnickers exclaimed that it was a dangerous area for flat tires, that the chauffeur surely could have been more careful. Pronob's driver, they suddenly recalled, was Moslem. They sat on leather-topped *morahs* by the roadside while a servant poured them buttermilk from a thermos. "Oh dear! Right in the heart of Darjipara! Why did this have to happen?" Darjipara was Moslem.

Sanjay and Pronob, anxious to show off, proposed they all go over to a lorry-drivers' teashop. But they were quickly put in their places by the girls. "What nonsense! You chaps must think we're the Rock of Gibraltar! That's the surest way to get cholera and jaundice and whatnot."

Nilima, temporarily exposed to the stares of cyclists and pedestrians on Barrackpore Trunk Road, said, *"Eesh,* how dare they look at us like that?" and her sensitivity was appreciated by Pronob. Some of the older women spoke in whispers about the

Moslem onlookers who had crowded around to watch the chauffeur change the flat tire.

"Look how near to us they've come!"

"Such smelly people. I think I'm going to faint right now."

"One moment please. Can you faint in the car instead?"

"We ought to ban beef-eating. That's what makes them smell so foul."

"We people are withering and dying and these people are getting fat and oily. How come they never practice birth control?"

Tara listened quietly. She was not particularly disturbed by the whispered remarks; only the force of their sentiment startled her. She could muster little passion herself. Her own, fraught with explanations and constantly reviewed, seemed all too pale and perishable. She felt quite cut off from the fidgeting women on *morahs* and looked to see if her mother was complaining like the others. But Arati was busy counting bedrolls and bolsters on the roof of a car to make sure nothing had fallen off. Then Sanjay strolled up to the women. Tara saw his face darken with what a rival journalist had recently labeled his "pseudoliberal wrath." She heard him use English phrases like "communalism" and "race riots" and the older women scattered quickly to their cars. Tara wanted to explain to Sanjay that he was wrong to bully them with English words, that she knew he too was often malicious in his editorials. But when he appealed to her, she thought of David and his earnest magazines, and had to smile at Sanjay to show her approval. Meanwhile the chauffeur responsible for this panic and self-analysis among the picnickers prodded the slashed tire, spat forcefully on it and finally completed his job.

The excitement over the flat sustained everyone till they reached the factory premises of Banerjee & Thomas [Tobacco] Co., Ltd. The front gates of the factory were black and formidable. If the reports of Barrackpore residents were to be believed these gates were electrically wired. Three gatekeepers in khaki uniform stood at attention in one narrow kiosk. The gate and its keepers were frail and inoffensive, but the imagination of the lower-class neighbors, seeking abuse or release, had made of them a necessary nightmare.

As the procession approached, the three *durwans* leaped out of the kiosk and unlocked the chained and padlocked entrance while virile picnickers smoked impatiently in their cars. Inside the factory premises some laborers waved tiny posies of factory flowers; others pushed their children forward from behind the legs of their elders. Young women like Nilima and Reena were moved by the performance of the children. They threw coins at them from their windows and addressed them as "little darlings" to show their affection. Then the entire procession disappeared in the direction of the guest house.

The guest house was separated from the factory buildings and the animal sheds by a large artificial pond, dug by the original owner of the garden house at the express wishes of his widowed mother. Though the pond owed its origin to the whim of a rich old woman, its main function now was to shield the Bengal Tiger's guests from the curious eyes of his laborers. In the evenings the *durwans* swam in that pond in order to perform all necessary and religious ablutions. Over the years, three *durwans* had drowned while performing such ablutions. A small boat was tied to a tree near the steps of the *ghat*. It had been given to Tara as a birthday gift by an uncle who had devoted himself to punting on the Cam for one fearfully expensive term. The boat had sprung a leak and been useless from the start.

The pond was surrounded by a circular driveway, canopied by living arches of pink and orange bougainvillea creepers. The guest house itself was adequately shaded by sturdy mango and *devdaru* trees. The spot where the guest house now stood had once been a wild garden taken over by creepers, bushes, trees, strange snakes and birds. When Banerjee & Thomas [Tobacco] Co., Ltd. bought the garden house, they had to clear all that, even the prize magnolias, *champaks,* grapefruits and cobras. Occasionally, on the hottest days of the summer, snakes still slithered to the guest house patio, and had to have their heads smashed by the Bengal Tiger's brave *durwans.*

The guest house itself had been designed by a friend of a jovial shareholder. From the day of its formal inauguration, people had complained that the guest house was airless, almost claustrophobic, totally unsuited to hot weather. Later it had come out that the young "architect" was an Algerian candy salesman who had fled to India to escape the retribution of the F.L.N.

The patio of the guest house overlooked an outdoor swimming pool. It was a splendid-looking pool, with marble trim and a deep blue interior. It had just one drawback: a primitive drainage system which had been devised by the same candy seller. The beautiful pool was strictly out of bounds of *durwans* and laborers.

On the other side of the swimming pool was the recreation club, a small, separate building consisting of two rooms and a yard. The recreation club was flanked on two sides by a lawn-tennis court and a badminton court, both recent additions for the Company Executives' Recreation Association. No executive, however, seemed to want to cross the pond and play tennis or badminton there. It was sufficient for them to know such facilities existed and that the board of directors cared for their welfare.

The large band of picnickers burst on this scene of bungalows, gardens and water.

"Welcome! Welcome!" shouted the recreation officer, while the guests investigated their surroundings and the servants snatched bedrolls from the roofs of cars. "I am waiting since dawn! I cannot describe to you my pleasure!"

"What is this nonsense?" asked the Bengal Tiger. "Since dawn is too bad! I instructed head office we would be here ten-thirty eleven sharp."

"Poor Recreation-*babu!*" consoled Tara's mother. "What an unhappy mix-up!" She advised her husband to take the matter up with "the boys" at the head office.

"No, please. No mention. No scolding for head office boys. I myself have just arrived."

The recreation officer had a vigilant desire to please; pleasing he regarded as a point of honor.

To Tara's friends a picnic meant a great deal of sitting around in deep canvas chairs and grumbling about the weather. Distressed by this inertia, Tara tried to interest Pronob, Sanjay and Nilima in tennis. Pronob was dressed for tennis, she thought, except for his absurd red ascot. He kept slapping his white-cottoned thighs as he told jokes about the recreation officer. The recreation officer, when pressed by Tara, could produce only two rackets, so Tara and Nilima had to return to the canvas chairs. The children of the guest house staff, ordered to act as ball boys for the day, blocked all view of the players. If it had been possible, thought Tara, the ball boys would have recovered the ball in midair.

Reena and Nilima did not appear to expect anything more from a picnic than the gratification of their desire for chilled mangoes and papayas. Everything was perfect, except for Tara, still in her mood, who sat beside them.

"What is this?" asked Nilima. "You are unwell? You look so hot and bothered." She suggested a swim to cool off. Besides, Nilima was anxious to show off the swimsuit Tara had brought her from New York.

She was soon joined by Sanjay, Pronob and Reena. But for

Tara swimming was no good either. She was depressed at this first sight of her friends in swimming attire. She felt there was something unnatural or absurdly heroic about their posture. The soft edges of their bottoms escaping the grip of the western bathing suit had no business being seen by servants. Nilima ran with flapping thighs around the pool and her swimsuit was duly admired by the others. Tara pleaded to be excused. She said she had never learned to swim though she had made several beginnings. Sanjay called her a "spoilsport" and offered to teach her.

The journalist was very handsome as he stood at the edge of the pool. He had a hairless brown chest and a charmingly brave air. "Just let yourself go," he said. "That's dead right. Relax. Walk toward me. No, no. Relax. How is it they didn't teach you to relax in America?"

Tara clung to the side of the pool, jumpy and cantankerous. The pool water, piped in from the bigger pond, was tepid and unwholesome. Water-logged twigs and mango leaves floated on the surface, and a surprising number of dead bugs. The blue bottom of the swimming pool tried its best to make the water seem attractive, and was embarrassed by its own failure.

Soon other picnickers jumped in and tried improbable stunts. "This is nothing. When we were kids we swam across rivers!" bragged their mothers, who had spent their childhoods in Pachapara. Now they were too old and dignified to wear bathing suits, and saris became transparent in water. "Swimming in pools is for the birds," said Hari Lal's granddaughter.

Tara sat on a shallow step and watched Sanjay show off. "You'll kill yourself! Why do you want to do a thing like that?"

"Don't dive! Don't dive! Tell him, someone!"

Her waist and thighs were washed by the sun-warmed water. Sanjay was standing on a giant cement fountain that was shaped like a lotus. He struck a comically romantic pose.

"Look at me!" he shouted to her. He probably meant look, what a good sport I am, look at my body, at this model of Bengali culture. Then, gleaming, hairless and brown, he leaped and hit the water.

"He'll kill himself!" screamed his mother.

"How he dares! What a daredevil!"

"Why isn't he coming up?"

"Sanjay, are you all right?"

This crisis gave Tara ghoulish pleasure. Was she about to experience a tragic accident? Would Sanjay suddenly drown just to please her? David was not capable of such extravagant emotion. He would consider fooling around on top of giant cement lotuses quite ridiculous. She thought this freak happening would permanently affect her attitude toward the group.

"Poor Tara is hysterical! Someone get the factory doctor!"

The guest house servants appeared on the patio. "Lunch is ready," they said.

"Shut up, you idiots! How is it servants have no feelings anymore?" sighed Nilima.

"Sanjay-*baba is* drowning," Reena explained to everyone.

Then the journalist erupted from the water, hair and shoulders plastered with soggy leaves. "I heard you! Fooled you that time, didn't I? Fooled every single one of you!"

"What a lark! He was only fooling us."

"Just trying to see if I was loved, that's all!"

"*Narayan! Narayan!* What a close shave! It's mentioned in his horoscope!" said his mother.

"Do you think you *are* loved?" asked Tara, but Sanjay did not hear her. He was still on the giant lotus, arms raised above his head, ready to take off.

"Lunch is ready," repeated the guest house servants.

Lunch was served on the patio. The Bengal Tiger insisted it was a very simple meal, that he had not had enough time to attend to the menu. But the flushed faces of the cooks and the noise of heavy utensils being scrubbed in the kitchen reassured the picnickers.

The guests attached heaps of fragrant snow-white Dehra Dun rice on English bone-china platters.

"How is it we do not get this kind of rice?"

"There are ways, my dear."

"And these beautiful platters? Tara brought them for you?"

Tara, who had brought few gifts for her parents, was distressed by this attention.

"I'm sorry," she began, "I really wasn't able . . ."

"You should see all the beautiful things she got us," interrupted her mother. Love was at times measured by gifts, and Tara and her parents knew they loved each other.

The rice was garnished with shrimps, peas, nuts and raisins. Surrounding the platters of rice was a ring of roast ducklings, which when alive had paddled in the factory's pond.

"We have madcap *Americawallah* doctor," laughed the Bengal Tiger. "Too strict and diet-conscious. You can blame him for the simple fare."

The roast duck was more spicy and delicious than any roast duck Tara had ever tasted. Ten crisp, brown birds sat in beds of cumin, coriander, ginger, tumeric and other more dangerous spices left unmentioned by the head cook of the guest house kitchen staff.

"Is everything satisfactory?" asked the ulcerous recreation officer. "Is De Souza's duck all right? These men can be so dumb sometimes, sir."

"Everything is perfect, Recreation-*babu*. How is it you cannot forget everything and eat like the rest of us?"

"But tell me truthfully, sir. Are the potatoes bouncy enough?"

"They're perfect, absolutely perfect. Grab a plate and try

one." The picnickers pushed six huge and greasy potatoes on a plate for the recreation officer.

Pronob and Sanjay were partial to the tossed salad which had been grown on the factory premises. But the older women considered their taste a sad aberration. "What is this nonsense that you fill yourselves with grass and leaves? Eat more roast duck!"

Tara watched the food disappear, not just the main dishes, but the incidentals, like shredded cucumber in spicy yoghurt, oily and wafer thin *papads,* pickles, chutneys, sweet and sour *dal.* She wondered at the frailness of her own stomach. She had never enjoyed her food like the others. She had never entered into the spirit of feasts. In New York she and David usually skipped lunch; David was given to fatness and dedicated to diets. Dinners were fixed on the run. David had been amused by her parents' chronicle of birthday menus in aerogrammes. How can they eat so much? It's obscene! he had said. But eating was not a matter for amusement, Tara realized. Nothing was merely amusing in Calcutta. She would have to write David that eating was a class protection, that it had been unfair of him to laugh.

Tara arranged lunch on her plate, choosing carefully from the display of colors, shapes and smells. The children, ball boys and Coke carriers of an earlier hour, had disappeared, no doubt waiting with their fathers in the kitchen for the platters to be returned so they too could pick them over and carry off their loot.

"You're very lucky to have a cook like De Souza," complimented the picnickers. "How much do you pay him? Two hundred rupees a month? *Plus* uniform?"

"Two hundred is not much," said the Bengal Tiger. "But he likes company service. You know how they feel nowadays about domestic work."

The men and women began to talk seriously about the servant crisis. They did not mind the servants' stealing a little from the day's grocery total, but they did mind their joining the Domestic Workers' Union. In their agitation they exchanged new stories about rape and riot. They reminded each other that Mrs. General Pumps Gupta had been abused twice on her way to the Metro Cinema in recent months.

"How is it the lower classes have such a good time? It's just us people who have to suffer!"

They grew shrill about labor problems in factories and tea gardens. They advised Pronob and his group to apply for immigration to Canada and America.

"Kanu! Nandi Lal!" shouted the recreation officer. "Bring out the dessert."

Tara, who had finished her rice *pilau* and duck, waited for further tragedy or danger. Sanjay in the swimming pool had provided an anticlimax. Some turning point was surely yet to occur. Tragedy, of course, was not uncommon in Calcutta. The newspapers were full of epidemics, collisions, fatal quarrels and starvation. Even murders, beheadings of landlords in front of their families. But now she looked for tragedy in closer quarters. Stretching before her was the vision of modern India. Though this was a Sunday the air was thick with industrial pollution. Across the pond, chimneys vomited smoke and fire. Tara fanned herself while analyzing her fears. Little splinters from the hand fan irritated her palms, which she had softened in childhood with fresh buffalo cream in the hope of an outstanding marriage. She had to admit her soft hands had not got her too far.

After the five separate dessert courses had been cleared, the picnickers belched with satisfaction and heartburn, then retired for the siesta hour.

"Good idea, sir," advised the recreation officer.

"You overfed us," admonished the Bengal Tiger. "The America-trained doctor will have a hundred *lakh* fits when he hears."

"But sir, what is this life if full of restraint, we have to watch and watch our weight?"

"Jolly good," said the picnickers. "Did you hear that? Recreation-*babu*'s got a sense of humor! He's playing games with

> *What is this life, if full of care,*
> *We have no time to stand and stare."*

"Like you, sirs, I learned it for my Inter-Science English Literature paper."

Everyone laughed, even those older women who had not been sent to college by their conservative fathers.

"Ah, those were the days," sighed an aging picnicker. "I remember learning it by heart. W. H. Davies, 'Leisure.'"

Temporarily their sense of panic, their racial and class fears disappeared. Delicately they reconstructed another Calcutta, one they longed to return to, more stable, less bitter. Buoyed by their memories of happier years, they retired indoors, the women confined to two rooms, the men to the rest of the guest house and the bar.

The afternoon sun, though sly and malcontent, had lost some of its earlier vigor. It deceived the picnickers into putting down their defenses so that they were no longer watchful of the landscape or of each other. Some actually fell asleep with mouths astonishingly open. Others dreamed of the days when they had written odes to snowdrops and skylarks. They slept on makeshift bedrolls and mattresses, no longer alarmed by the possibility of revolution in Calcutta.

While the picnickers slept, a thin little water snake, perhaps more curious than the others, wriggled through the network of drainage pipes and invaded the restricted pool. The water snake played with the mosquitoes on the surface. It ate the dead bugs that had escaped the nets of the alert *durwans*. It zigzagged among the mango leaves and twigs and swam in circles in the warm water. Then Tara thought she felt the floor move, and her own bedding, and this terrified her. "This is it!" said Tara. "This is the end. I'm shaking all over. Why don't the others wake up?"

She swung her narrow feet, pale brown and now slipperless, on the cement floor. She thought she should be close to some overwhelming knowledge in these last hours. Elegant bodies were all around her. She thought of Joyonto Roy Chowdhury dressed in British clothes of another era. The vibrations excited her. She felt ready for death. She'd been brought nearer to it all summer.

"I'm ready," she said, raising her arms in a theatrical gesture. She pleated her cotton sari over her breasts, and stepped over the bodies of picnickers.

As Tara emerged from her darkened sleeping quarters, she had to squint to avoid damaging her eyes in the glare. Everything appeared to be quite normal. The silence and the orderliness around pool and patio enraged her. She felt cheated. Her temples were cool, and the floor beneath her was once again firm. It had been just another anticlimax. She moved from chair to chair in case some meaning or point had been hidden by mistake under one of the cushions. Then over the marble edge of the swimming pool, she saw it. She saw that thing. She saw the snake.

"Help!" she screamed. "Help me, someone! Help!"

The little water snake had darted to the center of the pool.

"Mummy! Daddy! Help! Hurry and call the servants!"

Durwans armed with sticks and daggers arrived at once.

"Help!" the *durwans* shouted. "Where's Recreation-*babu?* Get him here quick! Hurry! Help!"

The commotion brought out most of the picnickers. They stood in groups on the patio, asking each other what possibly could have happened to cause such alarm.

"Hai hai! Someone must have drowned! I knew this would happen!"

"A picnic was a bad idea!"

Then they discovered the little snake.

"It'll go away," said the older women.

"We'll jump in and get it," offered Pronob and Sanjay as they stripped off their shirts.

At this point the recreation officer, who had been soothing his ulcers with antacid, arrived from his quarters. "No, sirs," he said to the two young men. "You will get wet." Then he turned to the two servants nearby. "Jump in quickly. Jump in and grab that filthy thing."

The servants took off their khaki factory uniforms and dove into the swimming pool of the guest house. It was an emergency after all.

"I have got it, sir," said one of the servants. "It's only a water snake. Quite harmless."

"Kill it!" screamed Tara. "Kill it! I can't stand snakes."

"No, no! It's bad to kill harmless snakes," answered the older women. "Its mate will return and take revenge on us."

The Bengal Tiger saved the situation. "Just throw the bloody snake in the big pond. It'll all be okay. And De Souza, don't just stand there like a statue. Make tea for all of us."

Order had been restored by the Bengal Tiger. The picnickers were satisfied the Bengal Tiger had done it again. He had removed the trouble to a safer place. He had not killed the snake.

"Why is it you became so hysterical?" the Bengal Tiger asked his daughter. "I think you don't eat enough. That's why you're nervous. I'm more and more convinced that your David isn't a provider like us people." He advised Tara to remain in Calcutta till she was at least ten pounds heavier.

The hungry picnickers ransacked all the ice chests for Coca-Cola and Fanta. They drained the guest house teapots. They did justice to De Souza's hard pink cakes and cream puffs.

"We're ready to go home," they said at last. "Thank you so much, Dr. Banerjee. It was an absolutely smashing picnic. How is it we do not do this more often?"

They tipped De Souza and the *durwans*. They lavished endearments on the servants' children. Then they piled into their cars.

"Why do I keep making a fool of myself?" Tara asked.

Part Three

1

"Eesh!" said Reena. "How the Catelli has changed!"

The statement was unfair. Very little had changed at the Catelli-Continental in the last fifteen years. The last European proprietor had added a thin band of national orange and green to the white turbans on the waiters. And in 1953, when a Marwari millionaire had bought the Catelli, the Prince Albert Room had been renamed the Ashoka Banquet *Ghar.*

"Goodness gracious!" said Reena. "The flowerpots have been rearranged."

"So what!" said Tara.

"Am I right in thinking you are being rude to me?"

"Yes."

"Such rudeness! It is not like you at all. Gosh! That's what happens when Bengali girls go to America."

Though Tara did not believe in intense friendships, she wanted Reena to understand her need for rest. She wanted to tell her friend that little things had begun to upset her, that of late she had been outraged by Calcutta, that there were too many people sprawled in alleys and storefronts and staircases. She longed for the Bengal of Satyajit Ray, children running through cool green spaces, aristocrats despairing in music rooms of empty palaces. She hated Calcutta because it had given her kids eating yoghurt off dirty sidewalks.

"How is it you've changed too much, Tara?" Reena asked. "I mean this is no moral judgment or anything, but you've become too self-centered and European."

So it had to come at last, thought Tara. A quarrel was about to occur. And over such an issue, imagine calling her of all people a European!

"That's a goddamn lie!"

"Goddamn?" asked Reena. "I've never heard of that one. I know damn by itself. Goddamn is worse?"

"It's a lie. You are lying about me right to my face. How can you do that? How dare you?"

Such passion did not frighten Reena. The nuns had certified her as a "thoroughly sensible girl." She was ready to cope with Tara's outrage. She wondered if "goddamn" was spelled with one *d* or two. "You see, how you always make things too personal? I was just making an objective analysis of you and you get all het up."

Tara felt painfully misunderstood. Her education had ruined her for quarrels and showdowns. No one, it was assumed, would dare to argue with a St. Blaise's girl. Now she was ready to retreat into grudges that would ferment over the years. "But it *is* personal! You're calling me mean and selfish. How can you expect me to be perfectly calm?"

"Well, you *are* a goddamn egoist. Don't you remember the way you reacted to those children on Park Street? They were just sitting and eating and you had the goddamn cheek to turn it into something personal."

"Don't *you* think of beggars as your responsibility?"

"Why should I, you silly-billy? They're paid professionals, probably paid by a big, fat goddamn Marwari."

"Doesn't it bother you that someone's hired these children to beg?"

"It doesn't bother me *personally*, no. I always give alms."

Tara wanted to go on with the argument, she felt she owed it to herself and to David to go on, but she was alarmed by Reena's distortions.

"Why are you always thinking about yourself?" continued Reena. "Why don't you worry about the suffering of your friends, for instance?"

"My friends suffer?"

"What do you think? Of course they do. As proof I'll tell you a secret about Pronob."

On this trip Tara had discovered moods in Pronob that were quite out of keeping with the moods of the group. He was angry quite often or impatient with the endless coffee sessions at Moonlight, Venetia or Kapoor's. He fumed at having to accept the existence of workers' unions. He said things had been much easier for businessmen when his father was young.

"I think Pronob is in love with Nilima," said Reena. "I've seen him eye-make at her on several occasions."

Tara had not been prepared for this secret.

"That's all?" she asked, deflating the conspiratorial look on Reena's face.

"You are not satisfied with Pronob's eye-making? You want him to be downright lecherous. My God! You are a real fuss-pot."

It was the word "fusspot" that calmed Tara. What a curious tie language was! She had forgotten so many Indian-English words she had once used with her friends. It would have been treacherous to quarrel with Reena after that.

And so they spoke of Pronob's meetings with the Jaycees and hoped the guest list for American exchange students had been finalized for the year. And they recalled other foreign house-guests Pronob had billeted with them in the past.

"Do you remember when we took the whole Australian bunch to Kolaghat?"

"The toilet paper incident?"

"That was really priceless! Wow! Those Australian boys shouting 'Paper! Paper!' and our village servants chasing them in the woods with 'No paper, no paper, only water, sir.'"

The plight of the Australians had seemed uncontrollably funny to the girls at the time. But, in between paroxysms now, she thought of her panic at having to open a milk carton at Horn and Hardart her first night in America. What terror she had felt when faced by machines containing food, machines she was sure she could not operate, or worse still did not dare!

"Serves them right for wanting to see the *real* India," giggled Reena. "These foreigners just want to take snaps of bullock carts and garbage dumps. They're not satisfied with modern people like us."

Tara wondered what David would do if he ever came to India. He was not like her. Would he sling his camera like other Americans and photograph beggars in Shambazar, squatters in Tollygunge, prostitutes in Free School Street, would he try to capture in color the pain of Calcutta? She thought he would pass over the obvious. Instead he would analyze her life and her friends in the lens of his Minolta. He would group the family carefully, Mummy in new cotton sari on cane chair, Daddy in "bush coat" beside her, she herself on a *morah* in dead center, with servants, maids, and chauffeur in the background smiling fixedly at the camera. He would go with her to the Calcutta Club, take pictures of doctors and lawyers playing canasta. He would explode his flash bulbs at Pronob's parties, and regret he did not own a tape recorder. No, she feared, he was wiser than she cared to admit to herself. Perhaps he would not do these things either. He would land unannounced at Howrah Station and say to the coolie wearing a number, I'd like to see the real India. None of this, of course, helped her relations with Reena.

Afraid she might become hysterical at the Catelli or that she might resort to bitter remarks about friends who loved her, Tara returned to the problems of Pronob and the Jaycees, who had to find homes for eighteen teen-age guests from America. I must get busy, she told herself. I must try to care.

"I'd be very happy to help you in any way I can when your guest is here. Do you know where he's from?"

"Los Angeles. He has a nice Irish name. McDowell."

"In the States you can't always tell. It's not like here."

There it was again, the envy for Reena's world that was more stable, more predictable than hers. A Banerjee in that world could only be a Bengali Brahmin, no room for nasty surprises. Her instinct was to say something mean that would ruin Reena's confidence in herself, that would make her see that Calcutta could no longer support girls like her.

"I'm sure he's Irish. How can a McDowell be anything else? In any case, I'm willing to take my chances with this boy rather than two girls from Columbus, Ohio."

"What does your mother feel about all this?"

"Come on, you know her. Of course, she expects disaster. She thinks I'll follow your example and marry an American *mleccha.*"

And again that bitterness, that instinct for destruction of smug people like Reena. She had never thought of David as a *mleccha,* an outcaste, not good enough for girls like Reena. She was numb with anger against Reena's mother.

"I don't like that last remark. Look, Reena — how *dare* you call David a *mleccha?* How dare your mother of all people talk like that about something that does not concern her?"

"What are you talking about? Of course my marriage concerns my mother."

"But how dare you call my husband a *mleccha?*"

"Don't get so excited, my dear. We are very modernized Indians, we don't give two hoots about caste. You should learn to face facts, that's all."

It was useless to pursue this anger. Reena and the others were surrounded by an impregnable wall of self-confidence. Through some weakness or fault, Tara had slipped outside. And reentry was barred.

"Would *you* marry a non-Brahmin?"

"Don't be silly. It's unthinkable that I should break my parents' hearts."

Amusing stories about Reena's mother helped to revive Tara. The poor woman was trying out stews and roasts on her family for fear McDowell would find curries uncivilized or ulcerous. She had stocked up on imported canned pork sausages, soups, packaged jelly crystal desserts. She had drawn a line only at beef; she was a good Hindu after all. Reena laughed louder than Tara, repeating details about her mother's efforts that she considered particularly foolish or extreme. The girls laughed with the relief of men who have just escaped disaster. While they laughed, clutching their stomachs, heaving masses of black hair, an elderly gentleman in blazer touched Tara's shoulder.

"Jolly good, Mrs. Cartwright," said the man. "Jolly good to see you again. I was afraid you had disappeared."

"Hello, Mr. Roy Chowdhury. I was so worried about *you*. Reena, I'd like you to meet Mr. Roy Chowdhury, who knows Daddy. This is Reena Mukherjee."

"How do you do, Miss Mukherjee. Do I know your father?"

"I haven't the slightest. It doesn't really matter."

After Reena had made her report, Tara knew Pronob and his group would say of her that she was crazy to talk to weird men in the Catelli-Continental. They would say to her wisely, Calcutta has changed, my girl; it's not safe to talk to any strangers, not even at a place as decent as the Continental. They would tell her violent stories of pickpockets and rape, and remind her again of poor Mrs. General Pumps Gupta at the Metro Cinema.

"I thought you would never come back to the Catelli. I thought, Mrs. Cartwright, you had perhaps disappeared."

"What a strange word to use. I don't think I like it at all. Tara, we really should be going now. We are supposed to join the rest of the crowd."

"It *is* a strange word," agreed Tara. "Sort of chilling, you know."

"Mysteries and death. Dear Mrs. Cartwright, do they excite you?"

Tara had no idea what the old man meant by his question. She looked to Reena for help but the girl was cleaning her thumbnails, her pruned eyebrows locked in an expression of ill humor.

"Are you too one of us?" he asked.

"One of you?"

"He means are you also a weirdo," whispered Reena.

"Yes, one of us, Mrs. Cartwright. An addict of violence and murder, in fiction I hasten to add."

Tara felt he was probably speaking in puns, her need to complicate was so great each time the old man appeared. The old man wearing a blazer in the summer heat harassed her notions of the plausible. He spoke knowledgeably of Hercule Poirot and Perry Mason, while Tara recalled a *tantric* singer near funeral pyres and a snake in Barrackpore swimming in the guest house waters.

"I'm sorry I left in such a hurry that day," she said. "I don't know what came over me."

"No need to apologize. You did the only sensible thing if you know what I mean."

"What's all this?" interrupted Reena. And Tara, noting the girl's sudden interest, foresaw stories and misunderstandings that would surround this encounter. There was no way she could explain that a quiet hour by the funeral *ghat* had conspired with the pain within her till she had been forced to exclaim that it was no use, that it was hopeless, that things in Calcutta would never get any better.

"For today, ladies," Tara heard the absurdly dapper man declare, "I have a very simple plan in mind."

"We don't have time for plans today, I'm afraid," said Tara. "But if we did, what had you in mind?" She herself did not like adventures, especially if they came to a bad end as they always seemed to in Calcutta. But she needed incidents to make much of in letters to David. David was painfully western; he still complained of her placidity. Things "happened" only when they began and ended. He wrote her that he worried she wasn't doing anything. He didn't mean working on Katherine Mansfield, but just reading and thinking and getting the most out of her vacation. He said he thought she spent too much time talking to bigots, why didn't she write him of things that really mattered?

"I'd like to take you to my place in Tollygunge."

"Mr. Roy Chowdhury, really!"

"What a lot of cheek he has!"

"What kind of girls do you take us for?" Reena confessed later that she had assumed at once the old man intended improper designs on them. After all they were both reasonably good-looking, almost beautiful if one overlooked small imperfections of teeth and ear.

"No, no, ladies. I'm gravely misunderstood. I mean no evil by my invitation."

Tara admitted in her letter to David that if she had been in New York and the old man an American, his invitation would have been merely sporting. But, at the Catelli-Continental, she shared the outrage that inflamed her companion.

"It's your fault," whispered Reena. "With your American husband, this chap thinks he can make these horrible proposals to us."

"It's *not* my fault. You're insulting my husband. You're insulting me."

"Ladies, ladies, please. Your whispering's giving me the jitters. I meant no harm at all." He explained he had a house and large compound in Tollygunge. He did not live there because it had been taken over by refugees and squatters. In any case, he had a roomy flat on Park Street, close to Kapoor's Restaurant. He thought it might amuse Mrs. Cartwright to drive with him across town to see his squatters. The other young lady, of course, was also most welcome.

"Is it a *bustee?*" asked Tara. She recalled frustrating moments at Vassar, when idealistic dormitory neighbors had asked her to describe the slums of India. "Are you taking us to see a *real bustee?*"

"It's a *bustee* of a sort."

"Do the squatters pay you rent?"

"Certainly not. I, dear lady, do not take from the poor."

Tara realized her last question had wounded the old man far more than her earlier suspicions about his honor. He stood in his sockless oxfords, the last insulted scion of a *zamindar* family, owner of tea estates in Assam, and he quivered. "To give, Mrs. Cartwright, is more pleasing than to receive."

He was pompous, of course. Besides, Reena and the others were quite right, Tara knew; Calcutta had become more dangerous than she remembered. It would be stupid to ride through the city with Mr. Roy Chowdhury to look at insolent strangers. But she wanted to trust the eccentric old man, who had without preliminaries shown her the funeral pyres.

"We've got to get going now," said Reena. "Really, my dear, don't you have any sense of time? We've got to rest for Sanjay's party tonight."

Tara's wish to trust the old man doubled with every obstacle offered by Reena. If Mr. Roy Chowdhury had been a little more cocky she might have responded differently. But she thought she could defend herself against any threat from a sockless man in a blazer. So she whispered to Reena that they had done the man an injustice, that good manners demanded they accompany him to Tollygunge.

"I want to go on record," Reena objected loudly, "as being totally opposed to this trip. It'll come to a bad end. I'm going for the sole purpose of protecting my friend here." Then she went to telephone Tara's and her own mother with invented excuses about going to the movies with an old St. Blaise's girl.

The trip to Tollygunge was preceded by the usual confusion about which car or cars to take. Tara was no longer bothered by such confusion. She had come to expect it; she assumed that even a phone call meant several bad connections in Calcutta. This, she guessed, was an extraordinary trip worthy of several arguments and false starts. In the end they agreed that they would all travel in Tara's Rover, while Joyonto's chauffeur would run an errand for the widowed Roy Chowdhury aunt, then go to his own *bustee* for lunch.

Tollygunge had once promised to be a splendid residential area, smarter than Ballygunge and without the upstart snobbery of New Alipore. The land had stretched for miles, unmarked by factory chimneys or swamps, broken only by groups of coconut trees. Friends of Tara's parents had bought land there in the forties. You should look into it, Banerjee-*babu,* they had advised, land is best investment, buy now before it all disappears. But the Bengal Tiger had procrastinated. Then had come the partition, and squatters, and finally riots.

The road to Tollygunge was circuitous. At first it was *pukka,* black and hardtopped, though very uneven, full of cracks and bumps. It crossed tramlines and railway tracks. It edged half-finished apartment houses where tubercular men shouted slogans from verandahs. Then, as it neared Joyonto's compound, the rod was *kutcha*, dry, brown and dusty before the monsoons. It was flanked by huts, cow sheds and stalls. The dust and squalor forced the young ladies from Camac Street to roll up their windows.

Had Tara visualized at the start of the journey this exposure to ugliness and danger, to viruses that stalked the street, to dogs and cows scrapping in garbage dumps, she would have refused Joyonto's invitation. She would have remained at the Catelli, sipping espresso and reading old issues of *The New Yorker*. Now she wondered what had made it so easy to come.

Finally when the vast compound of Joyonto Roy Chowdhury came into view, Tara thought her chauffeur had made a mistake, it seemed to her so dreary, a wall overgrown with weeds and grass. The opposite side of the street was more interesting. There was a movie house there, two bicycle shops hung with chains and wheels, and a teashop combined with medical clinic. Reena stared at the long line of moviegoers sitting on the sidewalk, and refused to get out of the car at first. Above the squatting moviegoers were giant posters of Hindi film stars, all looking sadly Jewish, Tara noticed; New York had tamed the fierce Semitic charms of Raj Kapoor and Waheeda Rehman. In India, Susie Goldberg would be a goddess. She slid out of her car and saw a very black man near her feet throwing kisses at a gigantic picture of Saira Banu in miniskirt. Then she heard Reena announce she would be sick if they did not go home at once.

Mr. Roy Chowdhury tried to head off Reena's sickness by offering to take the young women to the little teashop. Customers sat on uncomfortable wooden chairs, staring at a blackboard on which the proprietor had scrawled: *Try our Vegitable patty (Finest in World) . . . 4as. pr. pc. and Mutton Kofta Curry*

(*Extra Hot*) . . . *12as. per odr*. But Tara, who would have liked to say yes to show her friends she was sporting, feared the large flies clinging to tea rings on tables and found herself declining Joyonto's offer. Reena, who had not entertained the lunch invitation seriously, did not bother to answer at all. Only the chauffeur, who had been given lunch *baksheesh* by Tara, was anxious to taste the extra hot curry of mutton.

"Enough of detours then," snapped the old man. "Let's get to my squatters."

There were no formal gates, only a gap in the wall; also several holes in the wall, jagged and varied openings, where bricks had obviously been pried loose to build hovels or stalls.

"I'm sorry there isn't a gate," apologized the host. "The refugees arrived before the construction men had a chance to really get started."

Tara was bewildered by her first view of the large and dusty compound. She thought if she had been David she would have taken out notebook and pen and entered important little observations. All she saw was the obvious. Goats and cows grazing in the dust, dogs chasing the friskier children, men sleeping on string beds under a banyan tree. Children playing with mud beside a cracked tube well. Rows of hovels and huts.

"This was to have been my rose garden," Joyonto said.

The huts were made of canvas cloth, corrugated tin, asbestos sheets, bamboo poles, cardboard pieces and occasional bricks torn loose from compound walls. Posters were used as building material by the more desperate squatters. Saira Banu in ski slacks hung upside down on one wall. DEEPAK GHOSE LIBERATES, CAPITALISM ENSLAVES, announced handbills on many other walls. There were no doors to these hovels. Tara could imagine David asking quite naturally if he might go inside and take a look. But she did not dare look too closely at them herself. Though they were open, these homes seemed to her secretive, almost evil.

Tara concentrated on the children playing near a tube well. Most of them were naked. They threw themselves on the tube well's rusty arm, then ran to sit under its spout before the water trickled down. Some of them were holding bananas black with flies. Sometimes they put them down in the mud so they could play with the tube well. She saw a pretty girl in torn bloomers giggle as water sprayed her. She thought the girl would be perfect for adoption ads in western periodicals: *For only a dollar fifty a day you can make this beautiful Indian girl happy. She has no mother or father* . . . She wanted to adopt all the children playing with water.

"This is criminal!" said Reena. "What is this? How is it they do this to your private personal property?"

"I'm afraid there's nothing I can do about this," answered Joyonto.

Now Tara thought she was beginning to understand what Pronob had once called a pain in his stomach. She thought she now knew the meaning of Camac Street and its paraphernalia of spacious lawns, padlocks, chains and triple bolts.

"This is too much! Can't you throw them out? I mean bodily throw them out?"

"Eviction notices get torn up the moment they are served." Joyonto Roy Chowdhury seemed interested in other dramas. He nibbled the lapel of his blazer and walked ahead of the girls. "Come, Mrs. Cartwright. Come let me show you what should have been my vegetable garden."

Tara and Reena followed the goatlike old man past the tube well. *Bustee*-dwellers stared at them. Tara thought they had sly eyes and impudent ears. She thought she saw obsessive distrust on their faces — anger against people who were obviously not squatters.

"I told you we shouldn't have come, Tara. I told you it was dangerous to talk to strangers."

The young men of the *bustee* closed around the little party. They were shirtless and muscular. They had sun-bleached matted hair. They spat on the ground as they stared at the girls.

"Ladies, let me handle this my own way if you please," said Joyonto. Then he raised his manicured fingernails in an exaggerated show of despair. "The weather is unbearable, isn't it, sirs? I wish the rains would come."

It occurred to Tara that the next moment could very likely involve her in some tragedy or violence. She did not want to die, though getting hurt by vulgar hands and being left to bleed on the dusty yard would be much worse. She thought she loved David very much, and death or mutilation before she had told him that would be unbearable. If she died in the *bustee* she knew her parents would blame David. They would say that he was not like "us people," that he let his wife wander into danger. She thought again how much she loved David and how impossible it was to tell him that in the aerogrammes bought by the *durwans* of the Bengal Tiger.

"Are you the rent collector? Mister, just tell your boss we want to spit on his face," shouted a young man with a scar.

"Deepak Ghose liberates, capitalism enslaves," chorused the others.

"No," said the old man. "I am not the rent collector. Would I bring these two nice ladies with me to collect rent?"

Then the young men accused Joyonto of being a reporter. They struck matches to light their *biris* (Tara noticed the matches had been manufactured by Pronob's company), and they threatened to burn Calcutta. But Joyonto told them quietly that they were not reporters.

"How is that?" asked the young men. "You are really just looking around?" They offered, like tourist guides at official ruins, to show their *bustee* to the old man. They sang film songs as they led the way, even imitated love scenes between Raj Kapoor and Vijayantimala. They pushed aside children playing with a bucket of water. A naked ugly girl threw water on Tara and ran away giggling to the door of her hut.

"Chase her! Chase the *pugli!*" shouted the young men. "One *lakh* pardons. She's a *pugli,* she's mad."

"Don't worry," assured Joyonto. "It's nothing serious."

But Tara could not dismiss the incident as casually as the old man. There was to be no major drama, no sensational excitement, she understood that now. No big crises that she could later point to and say: that was when I became a totally different person. She would only suffer relentless anticlimaxes, which Joyonto would dismiss as nothing at all.

"I want to go back," said Tara. "I'm afraid I might catch a cold from this damp sari."

"But we have just begun, big sister," said the muscular young men. "You haven't yet seen the *pukka* house. The bathing area for ladies. The temple."

"I've seen enough, thank you," said Tara. "It's been a most unusual trip. Thank you very much."

Joyonto Roy Chowdhury, however, refused to let her go. He discarded good manners. "You can't leave," he insisted. "I'm not worried about my transportation back home. It is you I'm worried about."

Reena was a few feet ahead of them, notebook in hand, entering names and details she procured cunningly from the *bustee* children. She looked efficient and self-confident, an old man's secretary doing routine jobs for her boss.

"This compound, Mrs. Cartwright, was meant for eight separate mansions." Joyonto's voice was louder now, the English accent less pronounced. He was like a guide at some obscure, vastly sacred shrine, as if he were recounting history and not the failure of his own fortune. "There was to be a house for me, all on one floor, you understand. A museum, you understand, for all the things I bought in auctions."

Reena, still ahead, notebook in hand, had not missed the explanations of her host. "What about the other seven?" she asked.

Tara attributed Reena's new energy to her instinct for self-protection; it could not possibly be penance. Perhaps Reena felt if she could write it all down, she would calculate and avoid future confrontations.

"I'm partial to family compounds," Joyonto cried, yet louder. "The others were to be for my nephews and nephews-in-law."

Then the young men led the sightseers to a brick house. It was still incomplete. A hundred bamboo poles supported the second floor. But already the house looked dilapidated, fit for a demolition crew. A rusty cement mixer lay on its side before the house. Here too the walls were pocked with holes where loose bricks had been pulled away by other *bustee*-dwellers. The young men said that they would be honored to have the guests inspect this house.

The house was shaking with voices: of mothers scolding children, women fighting in the kitchen, young men wrestling in tiny rooms and old men smoking in open hallways. There must have been two families to each room. Others spilled out into the courtyard and the porches. The men and women who lived in this decaying brick house had more confidence than the inhabitants of huts and hovels. Some of their young men had enrolled in and dropped out of evening college. Some were businessmen who hawked safety pins and hair ribbons all day. They made the rules of the *bustee* and they enforced them.

"I was going to build a swimming pool right in front of this house," Joyonto said, now calmly.

"You were wise not to," said Tara.

Reena kicked the rusty cement mixer. Perhaps it confirmed to her that Joyonto was prodigal and a danger to her class. Perhaps she saw in that decaying machinery the end of her own dreams of technological progress. "It's criminal," she said. "If we start giving in to these people once there'll be no way to stop them."

Joyonto waited for her to finish, then turned to the rough young men. "It's been a satisfactory trip," he said, tipping them lavishly.

Though there was a note of finality in Joyonto's voice, the drama of the day had not been completed. It was time for the little party to leave. They had made excursions to the ladies' bathing area and the temple, and now they were going through the motions of farewell.

"We'll be late for Sanjay's party if we don't hurry," Reena said.

The squatters and their children were walking back with the visitors. For them, too, it had been a satisfactory day. Suddenly a little girl in faded party dress, her arms covered with muddy bandages, detached herself from the other children. She blocked Tara's way. Except for its size there was nothing childish in the little girl's face. It had already assumed the lines of disappointment that it would retain. The body, rectangular and skinny under the party dress, would no doubt thicken a little with unlovely handling but it was already the body of a stunted young woman. She came forward, shrill and angry, circling the visitors like a bird of prey till they responded with embarrassed endearments and nods of the head. The little girl raised her arms, making exit impossible for Tara and her friends. The arms quivered with hatred and Tara, who was only inches away, saw blood spreading on the bandage. There were sores on the little girl's legs, sores that oozed bloody pus with each shiver of hatred. How horrible, thought Tara, the kid's got leprosy, she's being eaten away!

"I want that!" screamed the little girl. "I want a sari just like that! I want that! I want that!"

It is harder to damage others than to damage oneself. Tara, who had been carefully trained to discipline mind and body by the nuns at St. Blaise's, lost her composure at that moment, and had to be dragged quickly to the Rover. No one was sure what exactly had happened. On going over the incident in Camac Street or at the Catelli-Continental the girls remembered outstanding details, but with each telling the chronology changed. Had Tara fallen on the child in order to beat her to silence? Or had the child thrown herself on Tara and tugged at her *dhakai* sari with bloody, poisonous hands? Reena insisted she had heard Tara scream, *Don't touch me, don't touch me!* She said that she had seen Tara claw like a maniac at the spot that the girl had soiled with her bandages. Tara only knew she had seen the muscular men pin down the offensive girl and fling her out of the room. A pail of water had been brought to Tara as a token of amendment. The mother of the little girl had threatened to beat her daughter. A five-rupee note had been offered guiltily to the child, and the money accepted on her behalf by two virile young men.

In the car, revived by smelling salts the faithful chauffeur kept in the glove compartment for just such emergencies, Tara had worried about making a fool of herself. "I'm sorry I ruined the trip for you people. I don't know what came over me. I saw that girl with leprosy and I just lost my head."

Reena had tried to comfort her friend. "It probably wasn't

leprosy! Don't worry about it. It's infectious only if you have an open wound. I've heard from my medical-college uncle leprosy is a very hard disease to catch."

Joyonto alone had maintained an indifferent silence.

Tara remembered being grateful to the chauffeur for taking charge of the situation. "I go straight to Camac Street double fast," the man had said. He had deposited the girls on the steps of the Bengal Tiger's house so that they could gaze at the deserted lawns, wander through the empty marble rooms, linger on the spacious verandahs, bathe themselves in the "English" style bathroom, and regain their composure before the maid brought them tea and sandwiches.

But more than anything else Tara remembered Reena just before they had parted from Joyonto in the car. Reena had drawn herself up like a tremulous Brahminical Joan of Arc. "Here are the names I took down, Mr. Roy Chowdhury. It's your duty to serve them new eviction notices. Good-bye."

2

A HUSBAND is a curious animal. His presence is discovered by a series of stratagems. Advertisements are inserted in newspapers like the *Calcutta Patrika* and the *Reader* of Bombay. "Wanted: suitable bridegroom for tall, very fair, excessively beautiful Bengali Brahmin girl of respectable family; age 20; groom must be foreign-returned, earning four-figure salary." Or: "Wanted: beautiful, very fair bride for brilliant Kayastha boy, 38, Class 1 govt. officer, father retd. High Court Justice. Only respectable parties need apply."

"You are not trying hard enough," Tara's mother had often complained to the Bengal Tiger while Tara had sat over her homework, pigtails sliding over the poems of Alice Meynell.

"There's plenty of time, don't worry. I always take care of everything, don't I?"

Tara recalled how this tableau had embarrassed her greatly in those days. She was anxious to fall in love, good heavens! There was nothing wrong with her. But marriage meant certain physical mysteries, centering, as best as she could determine, on or near the navel. She had been grateful that the Bengal Tiger, so fierce in the business world, had procrastinated in this small personal thing.

"You are supposed to wear out fourteen pairs of shoes looking for a *jamai*," Tara's mother had complained. "I'm afraid you're taking your responsibilities too lightly. You'll live to regret it."

"How is it you want to part with Taramoni?" the Bengal Tiger had countered. "Finding suitable match is man's job. Leave me alone or else."

These conversations always ended in arguments or headaches. A few months before Tara left for Vassar things had come to such a pass that her mother would prepare debates, practicing her speech in the privacy of the prayer room with prime opening sentences and calls on the gods for reinforcement. Then she would cook persuasive meals for the Bengal Tiger and finally broach the subject of marriage.

The groom is an easy target. He waits in his room after a day at the office and a shower and light refreshment, for female relatives to bring him photographs of beautiful women. He scrutinizes the faces, tensed by strong lights, not smiling for that would be mistaken for boldness, nor yet really glum for that would be taken as a sour disposition. Do you like this one? The father is a high court judge, the women whisper. Or what about this one? Her father is a civil servant. No, he replies with studied calm, her nose is too long, and that girl has no breasts.

When the choice is made and the bargaining over furniture, ornaments, number of towels to be given, sheets and pillowcases, underwear for the groom, clothes for the female relatives, all settled with maximum discontent, then the Brahmin priest appears with the tools of his trade. And after a fire has been lit, and the gods appealed to, and the bridal couples' clothes joined in a knot amidst applause from witnesses, when the guests have been fed, and the servants tipped and scolded, when the children have fallen asleep in their party dresses, then the groom takes his bride, a total stranger, and rapes her on a brand new, flower-decked bed.

"Why don't we get a *ghar jamai?*" Tara's mother once said. "Some poor but honest boy, very brilliant of course. We could teach him about the business, and Tara would not have to go away."

"Shut up, Mummy. I do not need advice from a female!"

One day in Madison, sighting a young man in an elevator, Tara had murmured to herself, "My goodness! How easy, I'm in love!" and had completed her father's business. But a husband is a creature from whom one hides one's most precious secrets. Tara had been dutifully devious in her marriage. She had not divulged her fears of *mleccha* men. Did they bathe twice a day? Did they eat raw beef? Did they too have to hiccup and belch? The white foreigners she had talked to in Calcutta had been mainly diplomats or businessmen out for the evening in their best tropical dress, anxious to please, or at least careful not to offend. The tiresome Australians who had been driven to distraction by the absence of toilet paper in a village, she preferred to forget.

Now there would be no brilliant boys, no invitations, no priests, no fires, no blessings. She was a married woman, victim of a love match. David knew nothing of Calcutta, Camac Street, the rows of gods, the power and goodness of the Bengal Tiger. She could not trust herself to explain; some things could not be explained. The security of a traditional Bengali marriage could not be explained, not to David Cartwright, not by Tara Banerjee.

Toward the end of her second year in the States, when she'd been deep in the problems of Hawthorne and his scarlet woman, Tara had received an important communication from her father. The importance was obvious enough: her father had taken up all the space in the aerogramme, leaving no room for her mother, not even a line for the customary blessings for "all great success in your term papers and other brainy things."

We have made sound progress [the letter had said], regarding your marriage. There is one Dr. Amya Chakravorty, very fine boy, Ph.D. in Chemistry (Heidelberg), earning modest but promising salary from Govt. Boy's father is educated man, middle-class, not rich, a professor at the University, and a member of University Senate, but money thank goodness is not at all our problem.

Anyway, we have initiated serious talks through your Uncle Bibhuti (who unfortunately is still unemployed, by the way), and things appear to be going smoothly so far. However, all plans have not been finalized as yet. The main hurdles, boy's willingness for marriage and dowry settlement, have been already covered with all due satisfaction to parties concerned. We have shown your colored snap to the boy in question. We have no studio photograph of yourself, a grave oversight on our part, but with the grace of God, this snap you sent us (sitting with friends at Princeton Homecoming Game) has proved adequate. I myself do not care for it too much, you look like you are suffering from rigors of cold weather, but your Mummy says that one is the best.

Dr. Chakravorty, the prospective *jamai* under discussion, will be leaving for Chicago in three weeks' time. On some research-cum-training project. All your Mummy and I can say is that this opportunity is heaven-sent. We are modern progressive people, we do not in any way wish to force you into marriage. We shall leave the rest of this matter in your hands, and of course to Fate. The boy will come to see you for a weekend during next Xmas hols. If you both like each other then, then all will be well. We have already ascertained his favorable reaction to your snap, and have from his father more or less firm commitment.

Do not act with any undue haste, or any degree of unnaturalness. Whatever God does is for the best. Or as the lovely lady would say: Que será, será.

If you should decide in consultation with the boy in question, that this is it, then wire us immediately. You may get engaged on the spot, but no marriage. Preparations are being made here for grandest ever wedding ceremony. No holes barred! Needless to say all your relatives, big and small, rich and poor, close and near, are extremely excited. As is old Recreation-*babu* of the factory, who plans to supervise the feeding of the guests.

One small word of advice from your mother. She insists I add that you do not kill yourself with overstudy this semester or next. It is essential you try to look your best for the Xmas hols. No doubt you will get A grade in your papers without much effort anyway.

Que será, será. Take it easy. Drink plenty of milk in your daily diet. You do not know how lucky you are to have unadulterated food: America is indeed the land of milk and honey; if I were younger I would sell my business and emigrate to a poultry farm in the Midwest. Good-bye and Godbless.

P.S. Dr. Chakravorty is foreign-returned and very brilliant boy, everybody likes him. I shall relate to you small anecdote of his liveliness and intelligence. Your Mummy and I took him for dinner and heart-to-heart chat at Sun Sun Restaurant. He was full of jokes, making witty cracks. When it was time to order, the Chinese waiters tried to get us to buy huge quantities of each item, but the clever boy cut them short and ordered only two plates of each, because he knew the size of each plate was immense. The waiters were entirely cowed by Dr. Chakravorty. Your Mummy and I were favorably impressed by this touching incident.

The letter had thrown Tara into utter confusion. She could guess from the closing paragraphs of the letter that her parents wanted her to give up her studies for at least two months in case it ruined her perfect wrinkle-free complexion. At every possible opportunity she shut the door to her room and tried to study her old book on flower arrangement. As for singing, playing the *sitar* or cooking gourmet dishes, she felt she had been very inadequately trained.

"Que será, será!" she consoled herself.

In the affairs of the heart or marriage, there was no doubt that Tara at the time was incredibly inept. As it turned out, things did indeed disintegrate. But, at least on this one occasion, Tara was not to blame.

Dr. Chakravorty, the prospective *jamai* who had been promised future control of Banerjee and Thomas [Tobacco] Co., Ltd. as well as the boss's daughter, arrived in due time in Chicago. There he met a Polish girl from the South Side, a limping divorcée who was kind to him on his first day, who taught him to be aggressive, to desire not just position and wealth, but sex for the asking; who confessed one Sunday in November that she was pregnant, and whom he dutifully married.

"Que será, será," advised Tara's father when Professor Chakravorty of the Calcutta University's senate broke the news hesitantly to the Bengal Tiger.

"Yes," agreed Tara, returning to her essay on Hawthorne.

Now, bewildered in Camac Street, still unable to share her fears with the young man in the elevator, she wrote him a letter that she knew he would find exasperating.

It's hard to explain what's happening to me here, David. Or for that matter what's happening to the city itself. I don't know where to begin. There's no plot to talk about. Maybe that's the whole trouble, nothing really has happened.

Mummy and Daddy are fine. They're starting another diet. But the cook's gone crazy over the blender I brought home. In fact, so far we've blown two electric fuses.

Oh, this will interest you, I think. I saw a real *bustee* the other day. Mr. Roy Chowdhury, that's the old man who drinks coffee at the Catelli, took Reena and me to see his *bustee*. Absolutely incredible, David. I mean you can't imagine how horrible it was. Like seeing it at the movies or something, certainly not like the beggars everywhere on the streets. Anyway I don't think I want to talk about it. Enough to say that poverty is an art your people will never master.

The weather's absolutely beastly right now. My parents are talking about a week's hols. in Darjeeling (that's the hill station on the Himalayas, I must've mentioned it before), and I hope we can go very soon. Of course it'll be unbearably hot when we come back. Anyway, at least the rains shan't be far away.

Do you remember my friend Sanjay, the newspaper chap? Well, he had a beautiful piece on "The Denigration of My Beloved City: Calcutta" a few days ago. Really great. Unfortunately lacking in his usual wit, but so moving, I can't tell you. Would you like me to send you the clipping by air mail? If I can find the paper, that is — the maid here is neurotic about tidiness.

By the way, did I tell you the picnic to the factory was incredibly tedious? Even Pronob and his group failed to be their usual scintillating selves. Though Sanjay tried hard. I mean he pretended he was drowning in order to make us laugh. I had one terrible moment I must confess. A water snake managed to invade our swimming pool. No, I better not talk about this any further. A snake in a swimming pool, you'll say! Calcutta is a jungle! Of course, it is a jungle, but not in the way you're thinking. Just be glad you're not part of this mess. I don't think you could begin to comprehend these problems.

All this doesn't mean I'm undermining your hang-ups of course. But at least you people can go to your analyst and he can tell you what's the source of your problem. We can't do that. I haven't heard Daddy mention any psychiatrist friends, not one. Maybe we don't need them. Our mess is too complicated, I'm afraid.

I could go on and on, David, but I must stop now and arrange the flowers for tonight's dinner guests. I know you're saying right now how can I worry about flowers when people are dying on the streets of Calcutta, how can I be so callous, etc., I know that's exactly what you're saying to yourself. Well, all I can reply is that nothing my parents could give up would possibly change the life of the poor. India is not a banana republic, there aren't any landlord classes you could simply execute or exile. We're all involved in each other's fates.

Well, I really must stop now. There's no more space in the aerogramme. You can't imagine how I look forward to your letters, though they're not always as affectionate as I'd like them to be. No, I'm only joking, your letters are perfect. Good-bye. Look after yourself. Love, Tara.

So Tara confided secrets in her letters to her husband, but managed quite deftly not to give her own feelings away. She thought there was no way she could describe the visions that had failed her at the guest house picnic. Such events could not be described to David, who expected everything to have some meaning or point.

It was not a toppling or sliding of identities that Tara wanted to suggest to David, but an alarming new feeling that she was an apprentice to some great thing or power. If she were pressed to tell more precisely the nature of that power, she would have to remain silent. It was so vague, so pointless, so diffuse, this trip home to India.

The eccentricities of overseas mail service made it impossible for Tara's correspondence with David to follow any pattern of confession, reproof and rebuttal. Two days after she had mailed her letter to her husband, she received from him several angry letters.

The letters seemed to Tara to make the same points. David was outraged. He accused her of "stupid inanities," and "callousness." He thought the customs she praised merely degraded the poor in India. He had started to read Segal's book on India, and he wrote: "With Segal, I shudder." Tara had not heard of this book, and in passing she wondered if it meant David was having trouble with his fifth chapter. David wanted her to take a stand against injustice, against unemployment, hunger and bribery. He made horrible analogies between her Calcutta and Czarist Russia on the eve of revolution. He told her that he thought from the omissions in her letters that a bloody struggle was inevitable, that perhaps Calcutta did not deserve any better. In the face of such outrage Tara knew she could never tell David that the misery of her city was too immense and blurred to be listed and assailed one by one. That it was fatal to fight for justice; that it was better to remain passive and absorb all shocks as they came.

There were also occasional lines of local gossip in David's letters. Tara clung to them because they did not tax her conscience. She learned, with some malicious pleasure, that Susie had separated from Phil and that Phil had taken an instructor's job at Montana State; and that Susie had a part in "The Tragedy of Motherhood," which Tara assumed was guerrilla theater. Such news did not demand that she share her husband's faith in democracy. In the early months of marriage she had insisted rituals were useful and democracy not always the right answer. But finding that these objections exasperated David and fatigued her, she had given in smiling, not hearing another word. She put away the letters in her suitcase, and retired to the verandah. It was still unbearably hot, though the rest of the house had been clamped down under cool-smelling rose sprays and damp coconut coir blinds. She sat in the center of the Sears garden hammock, and traced leafy designs with her forefinger. The lizards were out in numbers, still and prehistoric, fastened to the walls of the verandah.

She thought about Calcutta. Not of the poor sleeping on main streets, dying on obscure thoroughfares. But of the consolation Calcutta offers. Life can be very pleasant here, thought Tara.

3

EVERY MORNING between yoga and ablutions, it was rumored among Bengalis in Calcutta, Mr. Tuntunwala repeated his dearest sentiment. "Heart's matters," he was believed to say as he held his breath for several seconds, "heart's matters are for idiots and women." Tara heard him express that sentiment late one evening by the steps of the boathouse at Dhakuria Club while Chinese lanterns threw red and yellow lights on his monkeyish little face.

Her presence at the club that evening was almost accidental. She had run into Sanjay at the Catelli-Continental and been asked to accompany him to the club for an exciting assignment. He was covering a political rally for the *Calcutta Observer;* it was to be a rally for P. K. Tuntunwala, who had recently emerged as the strongest conservative candidate. She gladly accompanied Sanjay, thinking how he had changed from witty assistant editor to mad prophet in the last few weeks. In his editorials he wept for Calcutta, *this cudgeled and bleeding city that brings me a taste of cannibalism and ashes.* He called P. K. Tuntunwala, Esq. *the hero of all heroes, the only savior who can pull us people out of the burning and monstrous mouth.* If Calcutta were to be saved, he often told the group, then all other candidates must fail.

On the way over to the club in his Fiat, Sanjay remarked to Tara, "If strength is love, and I believe it is, then Tuntunwala can love very, very surely."

The group did not quite share Sanjay's devotion to the political candidate. Pronob, for instance, laughed at the idea that Calcutta was nearing any violent catastrophe. Nor did he see Tuntunwala as a savior. "That man is money-minded, he'd charge too much," he usually added. "Look at the way he runs his factories and mills! Look at the way he slave-drives his workers! Of love he knows nothing; I can tell you he is a mistake."

Tara found all this talk about love quite disconcerting during a political campaign. She had expected "integrity" to be an issue, and "political acumen," even "personal magnetism and charisma" perhaps, but Sanjay and Pronob kept returning to love instead. On a wall outside the club, in fresher and more assertive white, one political slogan had effaced all others: MAO BRINGS DEATH, NIXON BRINGS LIFE.

The management of the Dhakuria Club had put up banners and posters for Tuntunwala's rally. GHOSE UNLEASHES EMOTION: TUNTUNWALA LEASHES FRUSTRATION. LANDOWNERS OF CALCUTTA UNITE! There were balloons and ribbons and a brass band that played "Three Coins in the Fountain." Tuntunwala himself displayed awesome energy greeting guests at the club's entrance, belching out his orders to bring out more ice cream and *papadoms,* scattering malicious exclamations against "Those *goondahs!* Those weritable hooligans!" and picking his teeth for the cameras.

His energy did not win over the entire crowd at the club's

pavilion. Some, like Pronob, remained suspicious or hostile, though they paid substantial sums to Tuntunwala's campaign fund. They regretted bitterly they could not find a savior within their own circle. They seized trivial incidents — the candidate's crude and clumsy way with silverware, his fractured Bengali and eccentric English, his insulting way with their aunts and cousins — to justify their hatred.

Sanjay was glad of this opportunity to meet the man he had decided would save Calcutta. He cornered the candidate between the boathouse and the pavilion and dramatically threw away the questionnaire his secretary had slipped into his briefcase. Tara, who had been held up on the pavilion by friends of her mother, ran down the path to the boathouse so she could join them. Sanjay's photographer had just finished posing the candidate beside an arrangement of Chinese lanterns.

"First of all, sir," said Sanjay, "let me ask you. What is your exact stand on redistribution of land?"

"Those who work hard can make paradise out of a desert, no?" Then, without pausing, he said, "Mrs. Cartwright, I'm so moved to see you here. You're beautiful as usual, especially when you're a little out of breath."

"What is your stand on the resettlement of refugees?" asked an old man from a Bengali newspaper.

"May I remind you," screamed Mr. Tuntunwala, "if you men get too tricky I shall cut off this interview this very second!"

Tara had been flattered by his aside to her. She was eager to help him. He was a man of such energy, so aggressive, so brittle and ferocious that next to him businessmen like Pronob seemed flabby. And the Bengal Tiger, she thought, what of my father? And she wanted to cry. She watched Tuntunwala whip out charts and clippings from the pocket of his vest to force a point. But she thought that of all the journalists present only Sanjay, pale and fanatical, would write of him as "the savior of the moment."

"And what, sir, is your position on cow slaughter?" asked Sanjay.

"Only those cows that deserve to be slaughtered should be slaughtered. When you find one, let us know, okay?"

"Why do you think *lakhs* and *lakhs* of people riot in Calcutta?" asked a young man from *The Rebel Speaks*, a weekly with a small circulation.

"Because there are *lakhs* and *lakhs* of chinless and morally weak persons today."

"But what of frustration, Mr. Tuntunwala?" persisted the young man. "I ask you, what of poverty and outrage?"

The young man's questions brought out all the ferocity of Tuntunwala's character. Shadows, deep and fierce, gathered in that fistlike face. Sanjay's photographer crouched with his camera ready to capture the candidate's wrath. So Tara, recovering the artful innocence she had been taught by the St. Blaise's nuns, asked her little question.

"What of love, Mr. Tuntunwala?" she asked softly. "What of the refugees and love?"

At first the candidate seemed pleased, as if he thought she were playing charming games with him. Then he picked his teeth with a show of arrogance and said, "Heart's matters, Mrs. Cartwright, are for idiots and women. I do not knowingly stray into heart's matters."

All of this was reported in the *Calcutta Observer*. "As for love," Sanjay wrote, "a question raised by an impudent, unaccredited western reporter, Mr. Tuntunwala had a single, clear, ringing response. The age of love has passed long ago," Sanjay rhapsodized. "The needs of Calcutta are for confidence, investment, and enforcement." Perhaps Sanjay, in his madness, believed it. Perhaps Tuntunwala, in a politician's privilege, had added it later. Perhaps Sanjay, in the presence of the candidate, had only heard Tara's Americanized voice. Tara was beginning to see it clearly. The campaign, the articles, the bitterness, were merely to confirm it. Pronob and his friends sipping lemonade at the club were bankrolling one doom to forestall another. But this, however near, was still to come.

Just then there were noises by the lily pool in the center of the club grounds. Little sparks went off. Pink and green and blue flames danced on the grass. Children who had been eating ice cream all evening clapped their hands and asked for more fireworks. Sanjay took notes for his paper. The man from *The Rebel Speaks* laughed.

"What is this thing?" demanded Tuntunwala. "Call out the special guards!"

Then there were more bangs, more flames and sparks. Women began to scream. A waiter switched off the verandah lights. There was only panic and confusion, children crying for their mothers, men trying to reach telephones in the dark. "Bombs!" shouted Pronob. "How dare those chaps plant bombs in the club!"

Tara was flung to the ground by Tuntunwala, who ordered her to crouch against an upturned boat for protection. She waited for the flash, the bone-shattering explosion that would end it all. They've won, she thought, amazed. She was praying. Then she opened her eyes, and saw Tuntunwala squatting in front of her. He seemed perfectly calm; in fact he seemed to welcome this opportunity to display new mastery. He instructed her to stay put until he reappeared. He yelled to the public not to worry — P. K. Tuntunwala was still alive, still in charge. Soon the lights had been restored. A waiter and the journalist from *The Rebel Speaks* were apprehended by the candidate's special guards. Tara was ordered to emerge from her hideout.

"To think, Mrs. Cartwright, you might have been killed because of my political career!"

When the police arrived Tuntunwala's bodyguards handed over the two alleged criminals. There were many helpful shoves and pushes from respectable campaign leaders as the police led the men away. Even the children wanted to get in the act. They took bony little swings at the handcuffed men. As the journalist was being pushed toward a truck, Tuntunwala excused himself from Tara and ran to block his path. To the accompaniment of flash bulbs, he threw away his toothpick and slapped the journalist in the face. Then the procession continued to the truck. The truck left for the police station.

A crowd had formed around the political candidate. This man is an enemy, thought Tara, savior or not. She had seen terrifying hate on his face the instant before he had slapped the young man from the newspaper, and now he was being praised for his courage. Sanjay had begun to tell her of the editorial he would write later that night. "Industrialist with spunk," he began. "Say what you will, the man has charisma." An older man from a Bengali-language daily kept irritating everyone with his suspicions that the bombs had been rigged by the campaign managers to insure the correct degree of drama. He too was led out of the club by a special bodyguard.

"If only I didn't believe in heart's matters," said Tara to Sanjay, who was too busy taking notes on the size of scorch marks on the grass to pay attention to her.

Two sticks of dynamite were found in the box. "Thank God they bungled the fuse," said one of the bodyguards.

"One moment, Mrs. Cartwright," called Tuntunwala from the club's pavilion. "Mr. Sanjay Basu will be shown much dastardly detail about tonight's attack. I suggest you take my car and a bodyguard home now. Who knows what else might happen here!"

Tuntunwala had not exaggerated the dangers of the club. In the early part of the summer when she had seen the rioters only from the roof of the Catelli-Continental she had thought life in Calcutta could be a succession of exciting confrontations. But now she was impressed by the city's physical dangers. Now after the bomb or fireworks at the pavilion, after the crouching and shivering in the boathouse, she understood the group's fierce desire for protection. She had seen enough; she was no longer curious. Between the boredom of the group and the newfound zealousness of Sanjay, there was deadness. She thought again of the old man in a blazer and she prayed for his preservation, and hers.

When Tuntunwala's car, chauffeur and bodyguard arrived for her at the club gates she was thankful that he wanted to protect her.

"Driver, take *memsahib* to Camac Street," ordered Tuntunwala. The unflattering light magnified the candidate's ferocious ugliness. Tara thought she saw him slowly bring down his left eyelid and wink at her.

4

REENA RECEIVED a picture of young McDowell a week before his arrival. To her astonishment Washington McDowell turned out to be black. She and her mother argued at great length about the diet of "the African," as her mother insisted on calling him. They were certain he was a ferocious beef-eater. In despair they telephoned Tara, who was expected to be an authority on all matters dealing with "Europeans," even black ones. "Ribs!" Tara informed them curtly, and then hung up.

Reena's mother was so upset she seriously considered calling off the whole thing. Especially since other families had gotten American boys who could sing movie songs like "Que Será, Será" and say a few phrases in imperfect Bengali to delight their host and hostess. She was not familiar with the ways of Africans, had only seen them in Tarzan movies, and now there was not enough time to learn.

Reena, of course, thought of herself as a great deal more sophisticated than her mother. Her mother had come from an orthodox family and had not gone to school past grade eight, but Reena was a St. Blaise's girl in addition to being modern. She'd read Conrad at St. Blaise's and tried to keep an open mind.

The day of Washington McDowell's visit to Calcutta coincided with a minor citywide riot. The price of rice had gone up overnight, and though no general strike had been declared it was rumored that the followers of Deepak Ghose would take to looting grocery stores and overturning cars. Bringing young McDowell home from the Dum Dum Airport would be both difficult and dangerous. Sanjay offered to use his influential friends and broadcast an appeal not to give a bad impression to important African dignitaries. But Tuntunwala suggested that such an appeal would be imprudent. The *durwans* of Camac Street where Tara and Reena were neighbors offered to accompany the *missybabas* to the airport. But the Bengal Tiger, who had come to feel *durwans* were useless in a violent city, instead taped two red crosses to Reena's Fiat and advised her father to pose as a doctor on call for that day. Reena's father borrowed a stethoscope, packed his wife, Reena and Tara in the back seat, and left for the airport at daybreak.

When the passengers finally arrived no one except perhaps Tara was prepared for the "Africanness" of the young McDowell. His hair grew in a foot-wide halo around his face. Tara tried to whisper the word "Afro," but Reena's family was too stunned to listen. He looked about sixteen and he seemed to the Indians to be at least eight feet tall. In truth he was six foot seven and still growing, a high school basketball star on scholarship to Berkeley. He had long legs like bamboo poles which were partially covered with jeans on which several messages had been scrawled. He wore a colorful Indian shirt and beads and a peace symbol.

"What is this thing that Pronob has given us?" asked Reena's mother as she sat tightly balled in a plastic armchair at the airport lounge.

The project officer, who was a Rotarian and a slight friend of Reena's father, brought young McDowell over to them.

"Hi!" shouted Washington McDowell. He called Reena's parents Mom and Pop from the first moment. The whole party was quickly supplied with Cokes by the project officer, who explained that Tara lived in New York and would be of "veritable and invaluable service" to McDowell. Then they were left to wait out the riot at the airport. The project officer himself had a meeting in town, and so intended to borrow a purser's uniform and sneak out in an airlines coach.

"We are very, very ashamed about this riot business," said Reena's father. "I cannot think what you must be feeling."

Young McDowell assured Mom and Pop and Reena that he thought the riots were a gas. They asked him the only questions they'd ever asked Americans — such as how did he like India? — and he told them that he couldn't take the heat. Everything in California was air-conditioned.

"What do you know of our culture?" Reena's mother asked.

It was, for the moment, an innocent question delivered like an accusation.

"I knew an Indian cat back in school used to groove on Ravi Shankar records. Little guy blacker than I am — you know him?"

"Probably South Indian," said Tara.

"Name kinda like Submarine."

"Subramanian?" Tara asked.

"We are a very large country," said Reena's father. "This Subramanian chap is Madrasi. We have never even been to Madras it is so far away."

"India is a whole continent," Reena's mother put in, now more aggressively.

"Yeah — O.K." said Washington McDowell. "But all the way over on the plane they were asking me to sing Johnny Mathis."

"How silly they are," said Reena. Reena, through the mediumship of Carefree Kevin of Radio Ceylon, had once written a letter to Johnny Mathis. "Your voice is much deeper than Johnny Mathis's. You should sing Andy Williams's songs. Will you sing 'Moon River'?"

"Andy Williams, huh? Wait'll I play the records I brought."

Reena's mother kept prompting Tara to ask Washington McDowell if he liked chilled tomato cocktail. "You ask, please, you ask. He won't understand my English," the woman said each time in English. "Tell him we have very, very chilled tomato cocktail in the house. Tell him it'll be served under the garden umbrella as soon as we get home."

Reena's father called Pronob from the airport and was offered the assistance of a police escort. He turned the offer down, judging it to be too conspicuous and therefore potentially dangerous. Pronob then advised him to wait till four when the rioters were expected to disperse, and to form a convoy of host families for the ride to town.

Promptly at four the host families led by Reena's Fiat left Dum Dum. It was difficult to fit all of Washington McDowell into a packed Fiat. Reena's mother worried the African would get cramps. But she worried even more that Reena would be crushed indecently against a strange and gigantic male.

"Push over here," she directed her daughter. "There is too much room here." Reena found herself sitting on Tara's lap.

The street outside the airport looked wider than it had on the way out. It was deserted except for groups of mild youngsters playing cricket. Storefronts were pulled down and padlocked. Banks were protected by collapsible metal shutters. People watched anxiously from the windows of their homes. The ditches were dry and cracked at either side of the road. Once Tara believed she saw a man lying in the ditch but she thought it best not to exclaim in case it alarmed young McDowell.

In Shambazar the convoy ran into its first hint of trouble. The lead car was stopped by a band of fierce-looking youths. They made rude comments to Reena's mother, ripped the stethoscope off Reena's father and shouted, "*Masai* — that doesn't fool us. We weren't born yesterday, you know." "Hey, stop the car, man!" said Washington McDowell. Then he emerged, knees first, from the Fiat. They stared at him in wonder. They had never seen hair like a stiff halo. They had never seen clothes that carried slogans like a Shambazar wall. McDowell had a strange walk. His hips reached the eye level of the fierce-looking youngsters. They watched the loose rotation of McDowell's hips as he walked around the Fiat and shook hands with everyone. "Now you cats gotta get with it! I want some noise. I want some chanting, man. You guys gotta get a little class in your riots or else you ain't gettin' nowhere." He taught them to raise clenched fists and shout "Brown is beautiful!" He read them jokes from his sweatshirt and jeans and he was hysterically applauded.

"Right out!" the boys shouted.

"*On,* man. *On,*" said McDowell. "Now I want you all to come over here and apologize to Mom and Pop and Reena. You were right — he ain't no doctor."

One young man raised a penknife.

"No, man — cool it. Pop's brought me here all the way from America so's I can study how to help. How can I help if I don't even get home from the airport, huh?"

Washington McDowell's performance was repeated before each barricade. "*Arré* — this fellow is better than a Patton tank with our *goondahs,*" Reena's father beamed. By the time the Fiat had reached Camac Street Tara had the feeling that the whole city was standing with clenched fists and yelling "Right on, right out."

"We're very, very ashamed," apologized Reena's mother. "Tell him, Tara, tell him I cannot describe how ashamed I am about those horrible people. Tell him he'll get his chilled cocktail right away."

The servants in Reena's house, like most servants on Camac Street, were easy to shock. The female servants took one look at the new house guest and ran screaming inside the house. Reena's family allowed McDowell to pretend he had noticed nothing unusual about his reception. While Reena sat on the lawn and told the visitor she knew something about his people from having read *The Negro of the Narcissus* at St. Blaise's, her parents rushed to the kitchen to give the servants a scolding. It was an uncomfortable time for Tara. She had been asked to be a bridge between Washington McDowell and Camac Street during the crucial hours before dinner was served. Reena's father

had invited Tara's parents and Sanjay Basu to dinner to lighten
her load. Tara, who knew very few blacks in New York and was
invariably frightened by those she saw, wondered what further
conversation she could practice on young McDowell. He's *so*
American, she thought, even more than David. But the visitor
couldn't relate to her — she was just another Indian and the fact
of an apartment on the fringes of Harlem, an American husband
and passport, simply didn't register. She frightened him. But
he looked so relaxed and comfortable on Reena's lawn that she
found it hard to ask him small questions about his family or
hometown.

He said he was from L.A. "Watts?" she asked.

"Yeah," he said, and she realized too late that she'd offended
him.

It was impossible to be a bridge for anyone; she wished someone had made her duties clearer for the evening. Reena seemed
to be getting on extremely well on her own, urging the guest to
teach her new phrases and songs. Bridges had a way of clutter-
ing up the landscape.

After a while the dinner guests arrived. McDowell had tried
to spruce himself a bit for dinner by adding a colorful headband
to his Afro. The Bengal Tiger was the first to hold out his hand.

"Never mind," he said. "We're ordinary middle-class people.
For the next fortnight you'll be like our boy. No formalities,
no shyness."

Arati and Reena's mother looked pained and slightly embarrassed all evening as if they both suffered from menopausal nervous disorders. Reena's father tried to establish a party note by
reminiscing about his "student days in the foreign." He sang a
few bars from "Chattanooga Shoe Shine Boy" and stood up to do
his Bing Crosby imitation. But young McDowell appeared to be
on the verge of a headache, so "Pop" had to run up to get his

chest of homeopathic medicine instead of performing his emergency song-and-dance routine. Headaches were the plague of Camac Street society; Washington McDowell had gained some acceptance.

"Tara, you tell him homeopathic medicine is best in the world," said Reena's mother. "Tell him it's safe enough to give to pregnant women."

"I don't need no pills, thanks," said Washington McDowell.

"He doesn't need any pills," Sanjay repeated in case the others had not understood McDowell's accent.

The assistant editor of the *Calcutta Observer* was dressed in a three-button suit from Jordan Marsh, a raw-silk shirt, an English tie and Ganesh cuff links. He believed nice ties like that went a long way to save difficult situations. He had run out of his imported aftershave lotion, otherwise that nicety too would have been preserved. The young man had prepared very seriously for the evening at Reena's. In addition to dressing sharply he had honed his favorite opinions, elaborated them sedately on the way over, and now awaited the right pause to launch them. He felt his whole journalistic career had somehow been a preparation for this encounter. It was a good thing the black boy suffered from a headache. The boy had listened politely to the vulgar conversation of the older generation. Now he would seize the headache as his opportunity to withdraw with McDowell to the privacy of the verandah.

"Come, Washington. I think you need some fresher air."

The older men looked at him in relief. They lit their cigarettes and admired the smooth way the young editor had extricated them from a frightening situation. There was no need to struggle on in English.

They began a passionate and technical discussion of import restrictions and licenses.

"A marvelous idea!" agreed Reena as she followed Sanjay and McDowell to the verandah, leaving Tara no choice but to join her.

In the verandah outside Sanjay leaned against a bamboo trellis and tried to adjust his prepared ideas and delivery to the larger audience. He preferred a confidential man-to-man talk in which young McDowell would have given him the lowdown on America and he would have been frank, if necessary even bitter, in his comments about India and especially Calcutta. The boy had strange hair. Sanjay himself did not believe in long hair or careless manners or anything that detracted from a professional man's career. But the sight of McDowell's hair released him from his usual guardedness with foreigners. A man with hair like that could never be a *sahib,* and that in itself was pleasant.

The assistant editor stared shyly at the teen-age visitor, then handed him a clipping of a recent editorial he had written for his paper.

"I'd be delighted to have your opinion, my dear sir."

"We're in the midst of a bloodcurdling election campaign," explained Reena. "All those *goondahs* who stopped us are on the *other* side, of course."

Tara sensed the moment required her "bridging" functions. McDowell's sympathies were probably with the *goondahs.* It would be impossible to explain to Reena that Washington McDowell *was* the other side, that when he returned to Watts he would make fun of Camac Street girls like Reena, that one day at Berkeley perhaps he too would slash cars and riot. She was saved from refereeing the situation by Washington McDowell, who had started to stumble aloud through Sanjay's editorial.

"Some venerable gentlemen in this country have declared that democracy is suffering a crisis in Calcutta at present. That our democracy is in danger is an indisputable fact. Those who are not convinced of the dangerous crisis should be referred to the bizarre and inexplicable (fortunately foiled) violence during a recent campaign rally for the Independent Opposition candidate. It is inconceivable that in this day and age of Calcutta's enlightenment a militant majority should try to impose its fierce will on a responsible tax-paying minority. Does not a minority have rights? Does not the minority have feelings? We ask these painful questions because the vocal majority will not ask them. It is unjust to assume that wealth and indifference go hand in hand. Anyone who assumes that the multimillionaire Tuntunwala is disdainful of the have-nots should be referred to the fifty hospital beds he has donated to the Sarada Devi Ladies' Hospital, the specialized equipment to Physical Handicap Clinic, etc., and to the countless donations he has made to temples, schools, orphanages and other suchlike charities. The malicious campaign unleashed by certain other political figures to disfigure the reputation of Tuntunwala will only serve to strengthen this man's determination to succeed. Malice will not harm Tuntunwala, nor hate wither his tremendous energy."

Washington McDowell read through the clipping slowly and painfully, hesitating over occasional words and tugging at his Indian beads.

"Do you like it? I mean do you get it all?" Sanjay was anxious to explain the point and tone. He had come prepared to expand on topics like urban land reform, peaceful coexistence, unarmed neutrality, Five-Year Plans, the abuse of Hindus in East Pakistan. His mind was crowded with mathematical trivia about literacy percentages, crop increases, and bank interest rates, because Tara had warned him of the Americans' respect for statistics. Sheltered girls like Reena and Tara had no head for numbers. They could be counted on to be quite beautiful, intuitive and charming. Sometimes they could make almost brilliant comments on literature. But the responsibility for facts, dates and numbers rested with him alone. His head was

148 THE TIGER'S DAUGHTER

bursting with tabulated figures. Graphs, economic maps and charts had suddenly attained the proportions of a vision.

"I have *one* important question, man," Washington McDowell said solemnly, dropping his voice and placing a hand on Sanjay's shoulder. "Don't people here use any deodorants?"

Sanjay felt betrayed by the black visitor. He had been near a crisis — nowadays Calcutta brought him frequently close to crises — and he had hoped to give flesh to his new vision. A crisis would occur again, but he was sure the vision would disappear. Next time he would merely be a dogmatic journalist who stated facts with shrill emphasis and bored everyone with his ideas. No longer in a mood for international candor, he sat heavily in a canvas easy chair.

"We don't need deodorants, Washington," Reena said. "We people take three baths a day. We leave scents and deodorants to Europeans."

Washington McDowell looked to the right and left in the verandah, brought his knees up to his chin, shook his Afro head till the headband slipped below his ears, and giggled for the first time. Tara decided there was no point in telling McDowell that Reena had not meant her remark to be either amusing or malicious.

Sanjay rose stiffly from his easy chair. "You no doubt have questions about the caste system?" He did not intend to let the matter rest with deodorants and daily baths. "You no doubt think us primitive racialists because of our castes?" He was beginning to recover his British Council debating manner. "My dear sir, you probably think we are beastly toward our little *harijans*. But let me assure you, sir, that is an unfortunate and preposterous deception, let me assure you . . ."

"There is no caste system in India," interrupted Reena.

"It was technically abolished after the independence," added Tara.

Tara was disturbed that their talk had taken such a turn. It was going on longer than it should have. She wished Reena's servants would announce dinner. But Sanjay was pleased with the new flippant-yet-dignified personality he had resumed. He pressed on with more questions that could have been mistaken for answers.

"No doubt McDowell, my boy, you think of us as an undemocratic and underdeveloped nation? No doubt you think we're a race of philosophers and fire walkers? You think we'll never get on because we're poor at figures and facts?"

"Goodness," interrupted Reena. "Tonight you're really in form, Sanjay!"

"Well, let *me* ask you a serious question that I hope, sir, merits an honest answer. Is there discrimination in America?" Sanjay sank back in his chair, finger tips together as if he were praying for the return of his vision.

"Oh, isn't he too much! How to do anything with Sanjay when he gets in one of those moods!"

"You putting me on?" McDowell asked. The phrase, new for Reena, who devoured foreign colloquialisms and trivia, successfully diverted the conversation.

"Because racial discrimination was abolished after *our* independence. It says right there on the paper — All men are created equal. Yes, sir."

Tara felt sorry for Sanjay, who continued to sit with his finger tips together, a debater defeated by the refinement of his own words.

"There *is* discrimination, you know," Tara assured him. But it was no good. He had wanted to hear that admission from Washington McDowell. Having bungled her main duties for the evening she now concentrated on comforting the ruffled editor.

Reena and McDowell were arguing playfully in a corner. Exclamations reached Tara now and then. "You would really shoot? With a gun?" And from McDowell the words that had become so common. *Pigs. Honky.* Reena giggled with each new word.

Tara complimented Sanjay on his editorial and agreed enthusiastically that Tuntunwala was a forceful candidate. If only he could arrange a debate between Ghose and Tuntunwala!

"What you need, Sanjay," Tara explained, "is some kind of confrontation scene. You know what I mean? Some kind of drama involving Ghose and Tuntunwala. Very few witnesses, but a lot of coverage by reporters."

The sophisticated editor was not to be appeased by Tara's earnest suggestions. He felt from that evening on he would be a failure. He would not convince anyone with his words. Lizards scurried on the wall behind his chair. He pulled up a stake from a potted creeper and teased the lizards. "I am only a chronicler of events, my dear girl," Sanjay said slowly without looking at Tara. "You want me to manipulate destinies? I'll have to leave that to chaps like Tuntunwala."

By the time the "European" lentil soup was served, Reena had mastered the radical style, and Sanjay had begun to depress everyone with his comments. "This boy's not the joker he pretends to be," Sanjay repeated to anyone who would listen to him during dinner. "The boy knows the importance of my question. I've been keeping up with foreign magazines. I know discrimination still exists. He can't fool me. We aren't the only backward country!"

Reena's father admitted later that the dinner had not been a success.

A week after young McDowell's arrival in Calcutta Tara received a frantic call from Reena's mother.

"You are our lone *Americawali!* Can you come quickly right now? I cannot tell you over the phone the shame that has happened."

Tara canceled her plans for going to an Uttam Kumar movie with Nilima in order to help Reena's mother. She had accepted the responsibility of bridging problems between McDowell and his host family partially because it made her feel noble and competent and partially because he was familiar and American. The younger of the two *durwans* escorted her next door to Reena's house, and Tara was met on the lawn by the distraught woman.

"I thought you would try to hurry at least," complained Reena's mother. "Reena might come back any minute."

She led Tara through a series of halls and small rooms, up a narrow back staircase and through more small rooms into her private sitting room. Like Tara's house Reena's house was too large for the needs of the family, and looked permanently empty and middle-aged. Reena's older sister, who lived in a mining town near Jamshedpur, came once a year to visit with her two boys. But her boys were so well behaved that they too failed to make the house seem smaller or more cosy.

The sitting room, which Reena's mother had learned to call "my den" from an old issue of an American interior decorating magazine, was furnished exuberantly. Pink Sankhera sofas and chairs were burdened with overstuffed cushions in red, green, yellow and blue printed raw silk. Pale madras checks of blue and orange draped the windows and polka-dotted Swiss organza covered all tabletops. On the wall hung mounted prints of Mogul paintings, Radha and Krishna surrounded by monkeys and peacocks and framed scenic views of Lac Leman, Matterhorn and Lausanne.

"Have some mango nectar," ordered the distracted mother,

pointing to a brass tray full of light refreshment. "Go on, have some guavas or papayas."

Tara ate obediently as she waited for the catastrophe. The woman beside her appeared to be marshaling her emotions into place as she sat on the pink Sankhera sofa, a tightly bloused mother in despair.

"I need your advice," Reena's mother began in intimidating tones. "I have always loved Americans. I have told Reena's father I wish India could become the forty-ninth state in the U.S."

The pause was obviously for rhetorical effect. When Tara seemed about to interrupt she was waved to silence by a regally tragical gesture.

"I repeat again that I have always loved Americans. I say to you now in all frankness I stood by your mother when your wedding telegram arrived and everyone was crying."

"Just a minute," began Tara. "I want to discuss that."

But Reena's mother had no time that afternoon for small battles. She had reserved her phrases and resentments for some other drama. "I love all things American, yes. But I don't like that boy!"

Tara felt ill. This love of America by a plump Bengali mother on Camac Street was more than she could bear. She put her mango nectar down in a hurry and spilled some nectar on the frilly Swiss organza tablecloth.

"Don't worry about it. It doesn't matter at all. Today I've time only for very, very important matters."

"What's wrong with McDowell?"

"Reena calls him Wash!"

"Is that terribly bad?"

"What can be worse?" Reena's mother assumed she could not depend on Tara's sympathy, so she tried to work on Tara's guilt.

"Utter shame. Utter disgrace for us. How can I tell you how serious it is?"

The strategy obviously worked. Tara saw the hunched figure in the little pink sofa and she cursed herself for not warning Pronob and the project officer that foreigners could cause havoc in Camac Street, Calcutta. In recent weeks she had timidly observed Reena's mother at parties and had been shocked at the ignorance of the woman. No other word could describe the coarseness and vulgarity of her remarks. At first Tara had chosen words like "simple" or "naive," but gradually she had realized that Reena's mother had made a talisman out of her ignorance.

"Where's Reena?"

"How to conceal anything from you! I better explicitly explain."

"Explain what?"

"I suspect hanky-panky business between that boy and my girl!" This revelation was accompanied by unstifled gasps from the outraged maternal breast.

"I'm sorry but I still don't get it."

"You expect me to be crude? I'm saying that I fear Reena is in love with the African. I'm saying that I think they're up to no good."

The woman had heard whispered conversations between McDowell and Reena in the verandah; she claimed words like "sex" had floated to her chair hidden by a curtain.

"I blame myself, don't worry. What can a young girl do? She has her natural urges. I should have been more careful."

"But auntie, that's preposterous. Reena has no such urges."

"My Reena's a good girl. She's too innocent for such things. *Hai Bhagwan!* What if she's prematurely pregnant?"

The mother's self-berating was interrupted by the slamming

of a car door. "That boy is a traitor!" finished Reena's mother. That was to remain her final judgment. But before Reena walked in through the door of the small sitting room she prepared a gently tragic smile to greet the young woman.

Reena seemed more blithe and agile than Tara had ever seen her.

"Hello there," she said, surprised to see her mother alone with Tara. "Right on, both of you!"

"Where have you been?"

"I think we've lost him to the students, Mother. He said he was going to room with one of the boys at the coffee shop!"

"He's out of his mind! Call the project officer!"

"Seriously. They got all involved talking about pickets and things. And he just wandered off. He got lost. He said goodbye and just got lost, you know what I mean?"

Reena's mother had no intention of investigating for herself the meaning of the situation. She hurried out of the room to make urgent telephone calls to her husband. For a long time Tara sat lost. She tried to explain to Reena that young McDowell had been one of the *others* from the very beginning. Only his slogan, his outlandish appearance, his knowledge of music had deceived Reena. She tried to soften things for her friend. "In America a girl like you and a boy like McDowell would never have met — so it's natural that he's gone away."

"Power to the people," said Reena sadly.

Reena's mother had been wrong of course about the "hankypanky business." But the visit of Washington McDowell left other more permanent scars on Camac Street. The residents were pained by McDowell's easy desertion. Over gin and tonic they sometimes talked of it as "a thoughtless betrayal." Only Tara insisted it had not been thoughtless; it had been inevitable, a minimal act of gratitude from the other side.

Part Four

1

WHEN THE WEATHER in Calcutta turns beastly, when the air conditioning breaks down in efficient hotels like the Catelli, when dance combos in nightclubs halt their music so the drummer can wipe his chin, when bullocks in harness collapse in busy streets, then prominent Bengali families collect their children and their servants and vacation for a fortnight in Himalayan Darjeeling.

Hemmed in by mountain ranges, Darjeeling spreads itself a little higher each year till from a distance the newest hotels and houses are hardly visible among the forests. In the days of the British Raj, choleric Englishmen and their wives fled to Darjeeling at the first hint of insubordinate May. Homesick subalterns and captains had called it "the queen of hill stations" and had tried to make of its stubborn landscape a bit of England. The westernized Indian had shortened Darjeeling to Darj and endowed it with the comforts of a newer, stranger exile.

On clear mornings, viewed from a bend in the narrow-gauge railway tracks, Darjeeling does look vaguely European. Little wooden houses hang perilously from green crags, mountain flowers bloom in window boxes, ladies in tweed suits peer from behind lace curtains and schoolboys in gym shorts play rugby and cricket.

The town itself is clearly divided into two sections: the upper and the lower. The upper town is picturesque in a guidebook way. There are clubhouses, boarding schools, a mall edged by rows of wooden benches, a park for nursemaids and children, an observatory, luxury hotels and the chalets of very rich men from the plains. The upper town is landscaped by pine trees and mountain streams. Flowers are grown to prodigious size in the park by municipal workmen. On cool fresh mornings when the vacationer recalls the Calcutta of the sweltering plains, Upper Darjeeling seems to him not a bit of England but a bit of paradise instead.

The lower town is dominated by the bazaar. From the bazaar radiate dirty alleys and steep trails. It is not considered beautiful by fashionable Bengali men and women. But tourists eager to finish their rolls of film take the Cart Road down to Lower Darjeeling and spend the day examining stalls, monasteries, yogis and tribal dens. Here the trees have been cut down to make room for people and business. Mountain streams have been diverted to purify shops and hovels. There are no flowers here, only pretty weeds that cover the sides of occasional mountains. Anonymous holy men sit bent in improbable positions in the middle of the mountain trails. Near the bazaar are two Hindi movie houses and posters advising people to have no more than two children. The streets are crowded with tribal urchins in tattered jackets, bowlegged donkeys hauling firewood up steep mountain trails, and occasional palanquins for arthritic businessmen. The lower town looks like any other town in the plains, except that it is smaller and poorer and that it is high up in the Himalayan mountains.

2

NILIMA WAS THE FIRST in Pronob's group to leave for Darjeeling. Her family owned a modest house on Cart Road near the mall, but her father preferred to rent that house to tenants and occupy "a two-bedroom suite with fantastic view and all further amenities" at the Kinchen Janga Hotel. Pronob went up next. His father had returned from Benares for two weeks to consult a heart specialist, so Pronob took advantage of his presence in Calcutta to leave the Flame Co., Ltd. for a short spell. Pronob always stayed at the Chatterly Hotel though the food there was bad. Every year after the first two days he threatened to change hotels, but he never did, and the Chatterly management had grown very fond of him. Reena's and Tara's family left last of all. The Bengal Tiger had been busy addressing shareholders, and Reena's father liked company.

Hill stations were not recommended as resorts to the Bengal Tiger. He suffered from high blood pressure and fierce nosebleeds. But for two weeks in the year the Bengal Tiger was foolish and romantic. He loved the Himalayas; he had written three poems set in Darjeeling in his early twenties, and as a middle-aged man he returned every summer to those hills. Tara was happy at the thought of going up to Darjeeling. The small violence at the Dhakuria Club had unnerved her more than she cared to admit and her failure with Washington McDowell still tortured her with guilt. McDowell was rumored to be somewhere in Shambazar, safe from Rotarians, diarrhetic but active. She felt protected in the mountains. She heard her father say to the doctor over the phone, "Arré, doctor-babu, que será, será. If I must die then let me die in the mountains where the air at least is fresh," and Tara thought she too could die in Darjeeling quite happily.

The journey to Darjeeling was not a difficult one. It involved a short Dakota hop to Siliguri and then a steep climb in the airline's limousine. The morning that Tara went up to Darjeeling she thought the mountains were particularly splendid. The limousine curled past tribal women doing their laundry in mountain streams and dirty children running among pine trees, past a tiny train filled with Bengali families who sat on their baggage and waved back at them. Sometimes there were dynamite scars where mountains had been blown up to lay the tracks and narrow highways. The chauffeur occasionally pointed to boulders heaped at the side of the road and detailed the date of that landslide and the number of deaths or injuries it had caused.

Besides the families of Reena and Tara, the limousine carried a tall, white girl, a mustached old Englishman and his Anglo-Indian secretary. The two mothers whispered in Bengali throughout the journey. The Anglo-Indian secretary shivered in her thin cardigan, and the Englishman remained aloof and slightly malicious to the end. The tall white girl seemed friendly and exclaimed to herself all the way to Darjeeling. Tara felt sure the girl was American, but after her failure with young McDowell she was reluctant to respond to overtures by *sahibs*. The white girl was the first to be let out. The other passengers watched her leap out of the limousine with mannish energy, carry her own suitcase, and knock on the door of the Everest View Tourist Lodge, which seemed to them a low-class boarding house too close to the bazaar.

"She will not get fresh air there," said Arati. "Tara, why didn't you tell her that boarding house is too close to the bazaar? The poor girl will get sick!"

Then the limousine pulled up before the rock gardens of the Kinchen Janga Hotel, and coolies grabbed suitcases and picnic baskets.

"Sir," said the chauffeur to the evil-looking Englishman, who sat stiffly with his sick secretary in the front seat. "This is the first-class super-best hotel in Darjeeling. As good, sir, as the Mount Everest Hotel, the Pine-View, the Windermere and the Snow-Vista. *Sahib,* here running hot and cold water twenty-four hours per day, and all nice amenities. Plus famous view of Kinchenjunga range from bed every morning.

"The Chatterly please," said the evil-looking man. "And hurry."

The two families were welcomed by the hotel manager, who rushed outside at the sound of the limousine.

"*Arré arré*, Dr. Banerjee *sahib!* We're honored by your party's humble visit, sir! Make my hotel your home as long as you like. I have arranged special housie night for you people, and beauty contest and suchlike for the young ladies."

It was eight or nine years since Tara had been to Darjeeling. Scaling the mountain with foreigners in the airline's limousine, she had been very apprehensive. As a schoolgirl she had loved the hill station, had breathed deep like the others and murmured, "Oh how fresh the air is!" But this time things would no doubt be less perfect.

"Thank you, manager *sahib*," said Tara's mother. "The mountains are beautiful as always. In the mountains I feel God is physically present."

After tea in the main lounge, where Reena commented on the growing number of Marwaris in decent hotels, the girls telephoned Nilima and Pronob. Pronob sounded lonely, anxious for the latest news from the plains. He complained that the dining room in his hotel was musty and the meals too British and that he was a fool to come every year to Darjeeling. Nilima's mood was more ambiguous. She talked quickly on the telephone as if she were afraid that the others might try to ask her a question.

"We're in the west wing," Nilima said. "A simply marvelous suite overlooking the old palace. Ma wants me to do up my hair now because she's invited shoals of people before dinner and I'm supposed to impress them. We went to Tiger Hill last Sunday and that was simply super though we had to get up in the middle of the night to reach the right spot in time to see the sunrise. Just fantastic, I can't tell you what it was like, it was that great. I'll probably see you in the dining room tonight. We are table eight, don't forget." Then she hung up on her friends.

The two girls changed into pretty afternoon silk saris and worried that Nilima seemed to be avoiding them. They guessed that Nilima's mother was probably trying to clinch a marriage deal during the fortnight's holiday, when she could consult Nilima's father without competing with the family business. But they were astonished that Nilima refused to confide in them.

On the way to the mall after tea Reena and Tara thought they were passing the entire summer population of Darjeeling. Everyone had turned out in their holiday best to stroll near the mall and chat with people one avoided in the plains. There were women in bright georgettes and short woolen jackets. Men in tweed suits or gabardine raincoats left over from their student days in England or on the Continent. Children in ski slacks clinging to gnarled old horses and nursemaids in hand-me-down cardigans running behind them. Servants in summer liveries walking with solemn fat spaniels.

Tara was moved by her first full view of the hill station. The holidayers walked up and down the mall in solid groups of ten and twelve, or rode around the observatory on slow and retired racehorses. A band in singular but impressive uniform played "When Irish Eyes Are Smiling" from a permanent stand. Once she caught sight of Nilima talking earnestly to a bespectacled young man in a vest while a bevy of relatives from both sides stood self-consciously near a dry fountain ten feet away. Tara tried to catch Nilima's eye, and failed; so she called out to her friend and Reena waved. But Nilima pointedly ignored them.

"She's embarrassed by us!" Tara exploded. "What's the matter with her? Why is she avoiding us?"

"She's embarrassed of *you*, not me, my dear," Reena said. "She probably thinks that little man will run away if he finds out one of her friends arranged her own marriage."

Tara found both the snub and its explanation believable and infuriating. She was just an eccentric and imprudent creature whose marriage had barred her from sharing the full confidence of her St. Blaise's friends.

There had been a time, Tara remembered, when Darjeeling had meant quiet walks along mountain trails with Giribala the maid and Rajah the cocker. The Himalayan resort had released adolescent happiness; strolling to Ghum with Pronob and Reena and listening to Buddhist monks chant strange phrases. Once Darjeeling had meant not an annual ritual to be rigorously executed, but a time of escape from the inexorable plains.

"Hello there!" shouted a fat man in a navy beret as he eased the girls from the thick of the strollers to the edge of the mall. It was Pronob, barely recognizable in his winter dress. As a younger man he had wanted to study painting in Paris, but his father considered a term at Cambridge more prudent for a future match-firm magnate. His overcoat, beret, scarf and gloves were relics of that brief period at Cambridge and a Paris weekend. "Isn't this a crazy place?" He stood with his arms around his two friends.

"I can't think why we come here! You should see the jam at our hotel!"

So it had come again. They exchanged their annual regret at having come up, their disappointment with their hotels, their anger at the social improprieties of Calcutta acquaintances, of greetings unacknowledged and dining etiquette appallingly mismanaged. Tara invited Pronob to join them for the housie game later that evening and Pronob appeared delighted to accept. She wondered what prevented him from making new friends at his own hotel.

Suddenly the crowds parted directly in front of them, and a big redheaded girl in green pants and turtleneck sweater emerged like a tractor before them. Other vacationers had stopped walking and were staring fixedly at the white girl who had forced her way through their ranks.

"Hi!" she said, holding out her hand to Tara. "We came up together in the car this morning. I'm Antonia Whitehead."

It was hard for Tara to determine what was so startling about Antonia as she introduced herself and her friends. They had all seen white women before. There were still some little English-women in Darjeeling, all widows of ex-colonels who called India "bloody hell" but who had opted to stay on after India's independence. It was perhaps Antonia Whitehead's size that made her so different. And the athletic way she was so well put together. They had never seen such brutal health.

Antonia Whitehead led Pronob and the two girls out of the mall and the crowds parted again. They lingered for a moment near a bench where a cluster of Bengali children fell over each other trying to make room for them. But Antonia did not sit down; the pause, Tara realized, had been merely to emphasize some point the girl had made.

"Isn't this place great?" the American girl said, raising her arms in an extravagant gesture that made her little breasts jiggle inside the green turtleneck.

Weeks later, in response to a letter to the *Calcutta Observer*, Sanjay would write an impassioned editorial on Antonia Whitehead:

It has been said that she is really a blessing in disguise, that she is a missionary defrocked, that she is Deepak Ghose's special lady-friend. But I say to you she is dangerous. She is like a snake tightly coiled. I say to you get rid of her before she spreads further discontent. She talks in Shambazar of "democratization" and "politicization," of parity and socioeconomic balance. But I urge you Calcatians to throw out this perilous lady before it is too late.

But that would come weeks later, after the rains had come down, and the revolution had broken in earnest. In the mountains of Darjeeling, where one was close to the gods, Antonia Whitehead simply wanted to be a friend. That first afternoon, it was more early evening than afternoon, she accompanied Reena, Tara and Pronob to Smith's Super Snack Counter and bared her heart to the three Indians over faintly rank ham sandwiches.

The history of Antonia Whitehead was simple. She had been born in Buffalo and had lived there with her parents till her father died of a heart attack and her mother remarried. Her dislike of her stepfather had freed her for travel. At fifteen she had become a missing person, had found herself first in San Francisco, later in Arizona, still later in Singapore and finally in Calcutta, which she said she wanted to call home.

Pronob started to loosen up at Smith's Super Snack Counter. He leaned closer to the white girl than etiquette permitted and he asked a mildly flirtatious question. "And pray what brings a lovely lady like you to our country?"

"Oh, Pronob, what a silly question!" Reena exploded. "Of course we know she's here to seek peace and real happiness! Everyone comes here for that."

Antonia Whitehead laughed. Her laugh revealed gigantic, even teeth. Those teeth had no doubt been tamed by dentists in Buffalo, but next to dainty Reena's or Tara's they looked like the Himalayan ranges. "Reena, you're putting me on. I'm here," she said, turning seriously to Pronob and letting her red hair touch his Parisian beret, "really, I'm here because India needs help. The third world has to be roused to help itself."

And there it was, Tara realized. A small crisis without point perhaps, without emphasis or accent. But it was a crisis, distinct and serious, nevertheless. Pronob's face grew livid, though a girl from Buffalo could not be expected to notice changes of color under his brown smoothness. She resented the threat that Antonia Whitehead presented as she sat incomparably earnest and equine in a diner at Darjeeling. In this white girl with red hair Tara saw a faint rubbing of herself as she had been her first weeks in Calcutta, when her responses too had been impatient, menacing and equally innocent.

"I don't think you mean that," Pronob said. "I think you have a typically American sense of humor. I like a sense of humor. Will we see more of you after this day?"

"I'm dead serious, Pronob. And, of course, you'll see more of me. I thought you would never ask me for a date."

The matter of national need and individual utility rested there. Pronob offered to meet Antonia at the Everest View Tourist Lodge at seven, take her out to dinner at his hotel, then walk with her to the Kinchen Janga for an evening of housie and modest excitement.

"I don't like it," Tara confided to Reena as the girls returned to the hotel to change for dinner. "I *know* the type, believe me." And Reena had giggled. Like Washington McDowell, this American girl would supply her with phrases. "You poor silly-billy fusspot," she said.

3

TARA'S MISGIVINGS lasted all night; the next morning she decided it would be better if she left Pronob and Reena for a few hours and accompanied her mother to a local shrine instead. It was not as if she had not warned her friends. Their wit — or what was left of it — would have to see them through.

Tara's mother, given to religious dreams, had learned to consider shrines as physical extensions of her dreaming self. Her fondest hope was to see a vision while wide awake. Quite logically she had made temples her natural targets.

"Where is this shrine, Mummy?" Tara called from the tiny dressing room as she finished her preparations for a possible holy moment.

"Do you think your mother knows her right from her left? You'll have to ask people on the way," remarked the Bengal Tiger from the living room, where he was being massaged by a servant.

"All these years and he still thinks I'm ignorant!"

"You ask her what number house this shrine is. Go on, ask her what street and see if she knows."

"If God wants me to visit him today He'll find a way," said Arati. Then in a conspiratorial dash to the dressing room she told Tara she knew the shrine was in the lower town somewhere. "Are you sure you want to come with us?" The "us" represented a maidservant and herself. "If you go, the maid can stay back."

"Are you sure you really want to go?" the Bengal Tiger asked.

"Yes." After the bad starts at Aunt Jharna's, the afternoons at the Catelli, after an old man had shown her his ruins and a handcuffed young man had been slapped in the face, she thought she had little to lose. Calcutta was the deadliest city in the world; alarm and impatience were equally useless.

"I'm so happy that I can't describe it," her mother wept. "It was so hard to know from your letters your feelings."

The Bengal Tiger, who was still being pummeled by a frail servant with firm hands, was moved by the conversation he had with some difficulty overheard. "What is this? You still believe? You're our little girl again? How to express this fantastic happiness?" He leaped off the Victorian sofa where he had been lying face down, took out a sandalwood icon of Narayan from his overcoat pocket, and rubbed it gently against Tara's forehead.

The joy of her parents released Tara's poor atrophied senses. Her early encounters with religion had been restricted to little more than bedtime mythological tales, dressing up for the Durga Pujah feast days and hearing her friends recite the Act of Perfect Contrition at St. Blaise's. She knew any truly religious experience required self-abandon, even frenzy. She had committed herself to an unusually holy experience: a visit to the ashram of Mata Kananbala Devi, whom devotees came to see not only from all over India, but from America and England as well.

If through intuition or prophetic dream Tara's mother had divined the full importance of Tara's visit to the shrine, she would have insisted on consulting palmists and horoscopes to determine the most propitious instant for such an outing. She believed in good and bad days, even good and bad hours within good days. The Bengal Tiger often joked that Arati did not cut her toenails when the planets were in the wrong places. But Tara's mother was on a mission in Darjeeling. She abandoned herself to fate and called for a double palanquin so Tara and she could hurry to Mata Kananbala Devi's temporary residence.

The palanquin was like an uncovered sedan chair. It was carried by four *pahari* tribesmen. As a vehicle it was not particularly comfortable, but Arati's rheumatism was bad that morning, and the palanquin was the only alternative to walking.

"I feel sort of conspicuous in this thing, Mummy," Tara objected. "It's almost like a rickshaw, and I could never ride in a rickshaw."

"You are being sensitive." Her mother looked perfectly gracious in the palanquin, dwarfing porters and pillows. "Besides, you would be far more conspicuous running behind me and the coolies."

They set off uphill from the Kinchen Janga Hotel past little wooden houses where potty Englishwomen in wide-brimmed hats and garden gloves tended flowers, past little teashops above souvenir stalls and shops that sold photographic equipment, till finally the road widened, and the palanquin was at the mall.

"Let us go around the mall once," decided Tara's mother. "I'd like to say hello to my friends and perhaps invite someone to come with us to see the Mata."

"But I don't want to run into anyone I know when I'm in this awful thing!"

"You are just too sensitive," soothed her mother. "It is a sickness to worry too much about other people's feelings."

The older woman sat back among the cushions, which had a permanently stale odor. Every now and then she raised her hand and waved to old friends, or ordered the palanquin stopped so she could exchange comments about her health and Darjeeling's weather with acquaintances who seemed anxious to pay her homage.

Embarrassed and sullen, Tara began to realize that passers-by envied her mother and her. Their glances, their whispers, their sudden veering of bodies or horses, showed respect rather than scorn, and Tara was amazed. It had been so long since she'd been admired by anyone. She did not deserve that admiration; she had done nothing outstanding.

Their carriage was suddenly interrupted by explosive laughter at the mall. Antonia Whitehead in purple jumpsuit and felt hat was pointing to their palanquin and shaking Pronob by his lapels. Her gestures were amused, not angry, though the crowd in the mall considered such distinctions in the white girl unimportant. The holidayers stood in large messy groups, unwilling to get mixed up in any incident but eager to enjoy from a distance whatever drama the girl might generate.

"What's that?" Antonia Whitehead shouted. "What the hell are they riding, Pronob?"

"It is a palanquin," said Tara's mother with dignity. She had raised herself a little from the smelly cushions. "I'm sure you don't have it in the States."

Tara would have made some pitiful joke and blushed purplish brown in answer to Antonia's question. But her mother, though deeply offended by the white girl's laugh, had defended her palanquin and her country with simple restraint.

"You do look awfully funny in that thing, Tara," Pronob remarked. He sounded bitter, as if he had permitted himself to referee a match between unequals and was ashamed because he could anticipate the consequences.

"With my pains, you prefer she lets me walk? No cars are allowed, you know that."

"Where're you going in that rickshaw?" Antonia asked.

"It is not a rickshaw," Tara's mother objected. "It is a palanquin." (That evening, while the Kinchen Janga Band played "Around the World in Eighty Days," Arati would say of Antonia Whitehead: "How can you trust that girl? She looks like a boy. How can you trust a girl without hips?" But now she was more guarded.)

The destination of the palanquin was reluctantly disclosed by Tara. Her parents considered it unwise to talk of shrines and pilgrimages in front of foreigners. They'd not even mention their *kirtans* or *pujahs* in letters to her and David. In revealing the purpose of their ride in the palanquin Tara felt she was betraying her whole family.

"All faith leads to the same god. Faith is all that counts," said Arati simply.

Tara thought her disclosure would be greeted with silence or witty contempt. She waited for the jokes to come so she could look dignified like her mother and say firmly to the others that she thought God was within reach even in Darj and that she really must be on her way.

"Pronob, I want to see this shrine," said Antonia Whitehead.

"You will not like it at all," Arati said. "It's near the bazaar. Very hot and very dirty. Why don't you go and roller-skate? Exercising is good for your health."

In the end, however, the party of four set off on Cart Road down the side of the hill. The *paharis* sang as they carried the two women. They were followed by Antonia and Pronob on foot arguing affectionately, and an undetermined number of silent *pahari* children.

It took the coolies approximately twenty minutes to lead the procession down to the bazaar. Seeing a giant purple *memsahib* in their party, the coolies lingered in front of stalls where tribal women in braids sold ornaments.

The procession stopped once at a large confectioner's, where Tara's mother bought four dozen orange and black sweetmeats, then continued down the crowded alleys till they reached a bright pink house next to a sari shop.

"This is the shrine," Tara's mother said, making preparatory motions for descent. "This is where Kananbala Mata lives."

The four visitors pushed through the unlocked front door and found themselves in a chamber that resembled a Victorian drawing room rather than a Hindu shrine.

"Mummy, are you sure we are at the right address?"

"Of course, I'm sure. I'm good with facts and figures no matter what your daddy says. I got ninety-six percent in maths in my Matriculation Exam. I think the Mata doesn't live in a temple but in a private place."

The arrival of a Nepali servant with holy marks on his forehead reassured them. The servant seemed uncertain of the white girl, but when Antonia folded her hands in a *namaste,* he threw her obsequious glances. "You have come for *darshan* with the Mata Devi? This way please. I'm her *Chela* Number One, otherwise known as Chief *Chela.* Hand me your sweetmeats please, I will make certain the Mata Devi gets them."

Chief *Chela,* who suffered from a visible skin disease, grabbed the four confectioners' boxes from Arati's hand. Tara disliked physical defects and worried about germs polluting the sweetmeats, which the *chela* had taken to be blessed. The man led them to an inner, more austere chamber. This place was bare of furniture except for a wooden bed against a whitewashed wall. Large portraits of saints and deceased patrons covered the walls. These portraits were garlanded with tinseled marigolds. Rows of worshipers sat on an extravagantly patterned rug, and shook their bodies in time to a religious tune that existed in their heads. Some had brought their children; these children left puddles on the rug or ate dried fruits from a plate.

Tara's mother walked to a modest seat far from the empty bed, where Kananbala Mata would eventually relax and bless her audience. The worshipers who had arrived very early for the morning *darshan* welcomed the arrival of the newcomers as a diversionary incident. They tightened their haunches to make room for the new guests. They discussed Antonia quite freely, detailing in astonished tones the vagaries of her outward appearance.

Suddenly there came the sound of feet behind the curtained door, the jingling of gold bangles, and for a second everyone in the room fell silent. A woman appeared at the door, she was short and fair and very beautiful. She paused briefly at the entrance and a quickness passed from body to body. The worshipers forgot to stare at Antonia. They were no longer housewives, daughters or parents, no longer vulgar or complaining women. They rang little brass bells or blew conch shells or shouted, "*Ma, Ma, Mata!*" The woman stepped over the worshipers' hands and legs and took up her position between bolsters on the bed.

Tara found herself shouting "*Ma, Ma, Mata!*" with the rest. She found it easy suddenly to love everyone, even Antonia Whitehead, who was the only person standing in the entire room. It was not Kananbala Mata who moved her so much as the worshipers themselves. They stretched their arms toward the woman, whose skin was the color of saffron rice. They tried to touch her, her plump toes, her wet hair that dripped on the bolster and mattress. And some succeeded. The woman did not move at all after taking up her position on the wooden bed. She did not look at her followers, who now seemed convinced they too had shared her radiance. Kananbala Mata fixed her gaze on the iron bars of the window, beyond which was a view of the bazaar, and beyond that the mountains where God rested.

Warm and persistent tears rose in Tara's heart. She forgot her instinctive suspicions, her fears of misunderstandings and scenes, she forgot her guardedness and atrophy in that religious moment. "*Ma, Ma, Mata!*" she shouted with the rest. Then some rose to their feet. Others threw posies of mountain flowers in the direction of Kananbala's holiness.

"Chief *Chela* begs your blessing, Mata Devi. On behalf of

these worshipers, Chief *Chela* requests permission to present sweetmeats and other odds and ends."

Tara felt her mother's large body quiver beside her. She felt close to her mother, and to the other worshipers, close even to the *Chela* with the skin disease, so moving was the experience. Some new and reckless emotion made tiny incisions in her body, and forced her inhibitions to evaporate through the window that overlooked the mountains. Now, like her mother, she too believed in miracles and religious experiences. She knew men could walk on fire and sleep on beds of nails. *Click* went Antonia Whitehead's Instamatic camera. Antonia was getting it all down in true color so she could show it later to her friends. *Click, click* went Mata Kananbala's bangles as she hid her face from such homage.

"I'm just a housewife from East Bengal. Go home, you people, go home and worship yourselves."

"Chief *Chela* begs you, Mata Devi. Bless these sweetmeats and bowed heads."

"Go home and think of heart's matters. That's all I can say today."

The religious moment was over too quickly. Mata Kananbala officially blessed the gathering, canceled her afternoon *darshan* appointments, and left.

"Chief *Chela* bids all worshipers to partake of humble feast. All proceed to dining room with caution on your left."

In the dining room, paneled after some incongruous British style, the Hindu worshipers ate sweetmeats and peaches distributed by the Chief *Chela,* who took time off to scratch his diseased hands.

Antonia Whitehead had not been impressed. She said clearly and rather loudly that she had witnessed a depressing performance. What India needed, she exclaimed, was less religious excitement and more birth-control devices. She hated confusion of issues, she said. Indians should be more discerning. They should demand economic reforms and social upheavals and throw out the Chief *Chela* as pledge of future success.

"You're making fun of us," Arati interrupted. "What do you know of the beautiful feelings I had in that room? What can you understand of the love I just felt?"

"She didn't mean that as a personal insult, Mummy," Tara explained.

"I do not insult her. How dare she do this to me then?"

Antonia Whitehead would not be silenced. She spoke of the need for artesian wells in the rainless villages, of improved farming techniques and better-trained doctors and nurses.

"You shut up," shouted Tara's mother. "If I knew better English I would show you how you were misrepresenting us. You have no right to be in this place."

Tara came quickly to her mother's rescue. "Antonia, you are making an utter fool of yourself!"

She recalled again her own bad starts and mistakes. To Pronob and his group at the Catelli she must have seemed as naive and dangerous as Antonia. There was no way to warn the girl, no way they could be friends. "You're being quite idiotic about this thing," Tara repeated as Antonia turned away in disgust. Tara sensed that Pronob had given Antonia a wink, or at the least a fleeting smile.

4

BEAUTY CONTESTS were new at the Kinchen Janga Hotel. They had been introduced by Mr. Patel, the new manager, who had received his hotel training at Cornell. Since taking over the failing business, he had crowned a Holi Festival Queen, a Pan-Indian Hill Station Queen and a Queen of the Pujah Holidays.

The beauty contests did not help registration necessarily, but Mr. Patel believed in the establishment of traditions for his hotel. He hoped the Kinchen Janga would in time acquire an international reputation as a "fun place."

On the last Saturday before the June rains, Mr. Patel organized one of his many annual beauty contests. He hired old men, "refugees from terror in Tibet," he liked to inform his foreign clients, and gave them sandwich boards proclaiming a Miss Himalaya Contest.

"Will you invite me to the contest at your hotel tonight?" Pronob asked Tara. "I'd like to invite Antonia as my guest."

Tara, who bore reticent and ladylike grudges, gave him two tickets that had been issued as invitations to avoid complicated entertainment taxes.

"You don't expect her to win, do you?" teased Reena. "I didn't know you ever took out ugly women."

"She's not up too tight like you girls," Pronob retorted.

The mothers in Darjeeling were thrown into a panic by the promised beauty contest. Though they disapproved of such contests in principle, they worked very hard with creams and cucumbers and carrot juices to make their daughters lovelier. They regarded the event as a perfect opportunity to present a beautiful daughter to families on the market for brides, perfect because all preliminary negotiations could be handled with informality during the holidays.

The beauty contest should have been a happy and fruitful occasion for everyone. But a small incident on the afternoon of the contest almost ruined it for Tara.

It was a flimsy thing. Even Antonia Whitehead with her passion for accuracy could not reconstruct the chronology of those few disturbing seconds. When the Bengal Tiger was told of the incident he displayed unusual anger. "That Pronob is a no-good fool! Next time send for me quickly, let me handle it. That Pronob is fat and useless!" He assigned a servant to accompany Tara in the future whenever she went out of the hotel.

The afternoon began like any other. Tara accompanied Pronob and Antonia on horseback around the Observatory Hill, so they could admire the gray-blue beauty of the plains below, and then they struck out on little-used trails. That afternoon the riders discovered a lopsided grave erected by an Englishman for his "beloved friend," a Dalmatian, poisoned by a native servant. On the way back a band of rather scruffy holidayers in ill-fitting sweaters blocked their bridle path. At first Tara assumed the men had accidentally strayed off the sidewalk. But the holidayers came closer and closer, darting playfully between the three horses. They made rude comments about Tara and Antonia, blew them noisy kisses and slapped each other furiously on the back.

"You are so beautiful," shouted the frail and cunning holidayers in Bengali. "For love of you, we want to die. Come ride over us. Put us out of our misery, you arrogant, lovely women." They pretended to collapse with pain near Tara's horse, then picked themselves up and laughingly brushed her legs. From torn pockets they pulled out little cameras and took countless snapshots of Tara, who sat stiff and outraged on horseback.

"Do something!" Tara yelled at Pronob. "They can't take my picture! Strangers can't take my picture!"

The thought of those crude men lingering over her photograph, tracing the lines of her face, of her turtleneck and breeches, was more than she could bear. She wished she had not come to the mountains.

"Don't get so excited," cautioned Pronob. "There's probably no film in these cameras. They're just teasing you, old girl. If you ignore them, they'll get bored and go away."

The holidayers forgot Antonia. They aimed their cameras at Tara; some tried to separate her horse from the others. They tickled its tail with leafy branches. "Come, my beauty," they coaxed. "We want to see you in action."

A small hatless man touched her boot. Another managed a quick pat of the knee. Terrified horse and rider sprang into the thick of holidayers, who laughed and whistled all the louder as they jumped out of the way.

"Smile, please. Little more action."

"This camera's better. Please, sideface needed here."

"Blow a kiss here, lady. And one for my shy friend, it's his first visit to the mountains."

Two men tried to pull the reins out of Tara's hand while the others shouted obscene encouragement from the sidewalk.

"How dare you? How dare you?" Tara's shrill scream fanned the mountain sides. It was obvious Pronob and Antonia would not rescue her. She wondered what her father would have done if he had been present. Of course such disaster would not have occurred at all then.

Tara kicked one of the two men in the stomach. She lifted her foot again and again out of the stirrup, and kicked the muscular resilient abdomen. The men did not go away. They stood there, arrogant and sullen. Some shook their fists, others spat at the horse's head.

"You'll pay for this!" they screamed. "We never forget! We'll get all the likes of you! We'll be your judge and executioner! You won't have long to wait!" The men squeezed each other off the sidewalk and back on to the bridle path, so caught up were they in their dreams of revenge. Then Pronob took them by surprise. He charged in their midst, and they scattered down the sides of the mountain.

"Race back to the mall," he said over his shoulder to Tara.

He had no advice for Antonia. Antonia Whitehead could look after herself.

As they sped toward the mall, Tara and Pronob felt very close to each other. Pronob seemed to want to do something heroic for her; he was moved by her helplessness. Nasty things always happened to nice people, that was the trouble in Calcutta. He could think of half a dozen shrewish housewives, mothers and sisters of his friends, who deserved to be looted or raped, but only the quiet ones were assaulted. When Antonia later complained that she thought Tara had handled the incident disgracefully and viciously, Pronob was very short with her. He invited Tara to join Antonia and himself for tea with a rather pointed graciousness.

An hour later the Bengal Tiger recounted the story of abuse to his friends in the lounge of the Kinchen Janga Hotel. The friends were fathers themselves. They looked harassed in spite of the invigorating breezes. They went over the tragedy of Mrs. General Pumps Gupta, who had never quite recovered from her ill-treatment. They mentioned a new story about someone's cousin-in-law, who had been looted on Red Road, then left carless.

"Disgraceful," they chorused in helpless rage. "Our Calcutta has gone to a hell."

This incident prevented Tara from looking her best for the beauty contest. She could not be a candidate anyway; she was a married woman. Mr. Patel, the hotel manager, tried to compensate for the afternoon by selecting her as a judge for the contest.

That evening dinner was served early to give the waiters enough time to ready the dining hall for the evening spectacle. Young girls skipped their dessert and fruits and left early to change. Older men and women lingered over their cups of Nescafé and had to be practically ejected.

"The contest's really for non-Bengali girls," the older women exclaimed. "Ours are too shy."

"It was better in the olden days. No contest madness. Why, we did not see *him* till the wedding day."

"No, no, we must keep up with the times," some men objected. "The girls go to college now. They're much older than you were."

"That's the whole trouble. They're too old, they decide for themselves. That's how tragedies happen."

"At least there's still some respect for old age. My son, he has a son of his own now, but he'd never dare smoke in front of *him* or myself."

"Don't worry. Soon the left-of-leftists will teach our sons disrespect."

"It's already happened. Don't you know what happened to the Bengal Tiger's daughter today?"

"Well, she made a love match. Surely she can look after herself?"

Soon the band, made up of four retired nightclub musicians, began to tune their instruments and drown out those lingering, frightened voices. The musicians, Mr. Patel's third choice, had been hired considerably below the going rates, so they did not feel compelled to enjoy themselves. They opened the evening with a halfhearted rendition of "Que Será, Será," then eased themselves into "Green Sleeves" and "Goodnight, Irene."

A few Anglo-Indian boys in Elvis Presley hairstyles and girls wearing frilly party dresses got up to dance. They were quickly joined by some Punjabi couples and half a dozen progressive-looking Bengalis. Tara was not sure what was expected of her as a judge. She took out her notebook and pencil to make observations about possible queen candidates.

Antonia and Pronob arrived rather early and joined the Bengal Tiger's party. They made no reference to the riding mishap, though they did retell amusing stories about the dog's grave they had visited. Antonia looked particularly unfortunate in a dress. Earlier in the afternoon the turtleneck and pants had given her an air of alacrity; now she was swaddled muscularly in a chiffon evening dress. She had also experimented with Indian eye shadow, and her lips were brutally red. While Reena's father was going over his favorite story about the boarding house in London where he had stayed as a student, Antonia Whitehead pushed back her chair and embarrassed Pronob into inviting her to dance.

"I have known that boy's family since he was so high," said Reena's father. "I think I ought to tell him he is making a regrettable mistake."

"No, Daddy, I think he's just enjoying himself," answered Reena. "He can't be free with us Bengali girls like that. So he's taking advantage."

The Bengal Tiger's party watched the two young people as they walked closer to the platform where the halfhearted band was amusing itself. They were deeply moved, even the Bengal Tiger; they longed to warn young Pronob before he hurt himself, but they were afraid he would get angry or worse still would laugh at them.

Nilima and her family arrived quite early too, but they sat at a table far away. Nilima's hair was piled high above her head, giving her a fulsome Nefertiti effect. Little black tendrils, unhappily too curly, hung about her ears to soften the rectangular face. The face itself was tiny, turned sickly gray by white powder for the night of the contest. The eyelids, gently painted, made the eyes appear much larger than the face.

"What on earth are they doing to her?" exclaimed the Bengal Tiger.

The answer was simple. Nilima's mother, a somewhat un-subtle woman, had hoisted her daughter on a barstool high above the other diners, so Nilima would be seen by the parents of eligible Bengali men.

"She's going about it all wrong," Tara's mother said.

"Well, *you* didn't have to worry about such problems!" Reena's mother retorted.

That was true; her marriage had done her parents little good except to increase their fortitude. She heard her father immedi-ately come to the rescue with praise of David, calling him "a very, very brilliant boy and so lovable," though Reena's mother merely wriggled her bosom and turned away. Tara wondered if her father really meant what he was saying about David. Down in the plains, ten days before, she had heard him describe David as "such a good and lovable boy" to an audience of distant and disapproving relatives, while a servant in khaki shorts had rubbed his neck tense with tobacco problems. Now her father was following up the praise of David with loud and vigorous dreams about his old age.

"Yes, I'll sell the firm," the Bengal Tiger shouted. "It means nothing to me. I'll buy a poultry farm in America. I'll go to America. I have initiative. Taramoni and David will live with us and help. We'll have happy-go-lucky days again."

The dance music might have lessened the misery Tara felt as she heard her father's emotional rebuke to the vulgar woman. But the musicians were taking a break. They stood in a corner of the platform, smoking cheap little cigarettes and comparing callouses. The dancers, still full of unutilized energy, swayed noiselessly in twos during this enforced rest.

"What a dashed nuisance!" exploded Pronob. "Why must they quit playing when I'm just getting the hang of it?"

Only Antonia Whitehead was undisturbed by the musicians'

break. She had plans for a livelier evening than the band had provided. She led Pronob back to the table like a puppy on a leash, stroked his head once or twice, then walked purposefully to the microphone on the stage.

"What's she doing to our mike?" yelled the leader of the musicians. His assistants shook their frail and alarmed fists at Miss Whitehead. But Antonia was too busy trying to look sexy to be frightened by them.

"Please, please, dear lady," pleaded Mr. Patel, slipping tiny homeopathic pills into his mouth. He felt a responsibility toward his resident guests; the ugly girl in chiffon was likely to offend them.

"What's this? What's going to happen?" asked the dancers as they backed away from the stage.

In response to the whispered questions Antonia rubbed her fingers slowly over the straps of her evening dress, and let them slip a little so that even from that distance raw lines were revealed on each shoulder. Occasionally she brought her fingers to her hair, fluffed it slyly, then pressed a strand against her lips. She closed her eyes now and then, and rocked gently from side to side. It was an evil moment for the audience. The dancers and diners were stupefied, some staring greedily at the figure on the stage, others looking fixedly at the designs on their china plates. They were afraid of an unleashed energy; the swaying and rocking, they believed, was only the prologue to stranger events. And they waited for some miracle or sign to save them from this new threat.

The sign came very quickly. It came from the Bengal Tiger himself. "Sing, Miss Whitehead. Sing for us, please," he said.

"Bravo!" shouted the others. "Bravo! Sing, please. Accompaniment! Accompaniment!"

Antonia Whitehead straightened up on the stage. She became

efficient and businesslike at once, consulted the four musicians, hummed a few bars, then threw back her head and sang lustily. Her song was well received, and so she refused to surrender the mike, sang several more songs, and finally blew kisses from her perch at Mr. Patel and his guests.

"She's more diligent than those musicians," said the audience. "Surely Patel will give her a cut of those men's salary?" The band seized their instruments again, this time as if they would use their guitars and cellos to nudge the young woman off the stage. But Antonia gave them each a perfunctory little kiss and jumped to the floor by herself.

The audience bravoed her all over again, some playboy types even tried to squeeze her hand as she walked by their tables. The feelings of the Anglo-Indian dancers were closer to hero-worship than affection. In their cross-cultural eyes she was a dream made flesh. After Antonia's performance they felt anything was possible. They too might leap on the stage and seize the mike and force the Indian audience to listen. If Antonia had not been so far out of their reach, they would have hugged her, they thought, to show their gratitude.

"I can sing like that too, man," said Victoria Fernandez, the prettiest of the Anglo-Indian girls at the dance. "Man, my grandmother was the toast of London."

"Victoria, you sing like some kind of angel," agreed her friends. "If they saw you in England they'd make you a star in two days." They threw their thin and supple bodies into new, energetic dance steps.

"I'm going to the States, man. I'm going to save my moolah and buy a one-way ticket," all the young men said.

"They appreciate good singing there. Here my talents are quite unappreciated."

Mr. Patel dismissed his earlier apprehensions of the evening as quite unwarranted. He had a habit of cupping his pudgy hands over his mouth and shouting for attention whenever he wanted to address more than two of his guests. He could be seen on the stage now, cupping his hands. Tara feared the time for her to act as judge had arrived. She quickly took out a notebook from the purse she had bought at foolhardy expense from Saks Fifth Avenue to impress her Calcutta friends.

"Could I draw your humble minds to my direction, please," began Mr. Patel. "I remind you, ladies and gentlemen, tonight is the night of the Kinchen Janga Miss Himalaya Beauty Queen Contest. The winner of tonight's activities, that lucky young lady, will compete in the Pan-Hill-Station Deluxe Beauty Queen Contest."

The dancers on the floor pounded with their shoes and Mr. Patel had to restrain their gaiety with a look he reserved for obstreperous nonresident guests.

"We have decided to run this contest in a most democratic way. All men, no matter what age, will write the name of the most beautiful lady on a slip of white paper to be passed out by the waiters. Only ladies who are heavenly looking and unmarried, please. The judges will come with me, and count the slips when they have been collected . . ."

He read out the list of judges with appropriate flattering appositions for each name. Tara was listed as the "exquisite and intellectual daughter of very big industrial magnate." In addition to Tara, there was a Calcutta High Court judge, the wife of a Bengali diplomat, a heart specialist, and a Marwari real estate agent.

"The band will play dance music, and all heavenly ladies and their partners will please dance near the stage so we can get a good look before we cast our momentous votes."

Victoria Fernandez and her friends, buoyed up by their frilly petticoats and dresses, floated to the center of the dance floor. They executed difficult dance steps before the band had had a chance to warm up and really get started. They displayed certifiable self-confidence as they waited for the male guests to come up and find out their first names. Some Indian girls were also on the floor, progressive and tomboyish if hair and deportment could still be regarded as an Indian woman's inner index. They had allowed themselves to be led near the stage after nominal persuasion by male admirers and parents, and now they made a pleasing dynamo of energy and grace. But their western dance movements seemed lamentably related to *Bharat natyam* and *Kathakali,* which they had been taught by stern long-haired dancing masters since the age of nine or ten.

"What about the bathing suit bit?" Antonia Whitehead asked in a loud voice. "You can't have a real beauty contest in clothes like that."

Mr. Patel, who prided himself as an open-minded hotel manager, was upset by the suggestion. It sounded obscene to him; he wished he had not heard it, or better still that it had not been made. On the other hand, Miss Whitehead, he acknowledged, was a real American and could be expected to know how beauty contests were run; his professionalism was at stake.

"What should I do?" he asked the panel of judges.

"You could dismiss her case," advised the High Court judge.

"I think we should try not to be overtly rude to the foreign young lady," the diplomat's wife mediated. "We should, in my opinion, ignore her comments, and just carry on as if nothing has been said. You might also ask that stupid band to play a little louder, Mr. Patel. That'll cut down the possibilities of more such comments from nonresident guests."

"But why not a bathing suit contest?" Tara demanded. "That's a legitimate demand if you are going to judge a person's physical appearance."

"Really, Mrs. Cartwright. I think your years abroad have robbed you of feminine propriety or you are joking with us. You know as well as I do our modest Indian girls would not submit to such disgrace." The heart specialist was genuinely offended.

"No, no," shouted the Marwari real estate agent, who begged old editions of *Playboy* from his more westernized friends. "Let the girls wear bathing suits. The modest ones should not be in the contest anyway."

"But," said Mr. Patel, not wishing to take sides in spite of his prudish prejudices, "none of these ladies have their swimsuits with them. I'm sure they did not expect to swim tonight."

"Then let them wear their birthday suits. That suits me jolly okay." The Marwari's rejoinder, made a little too close to the microphone, carried to the audience and totally destroyed its illusions of beauty and love.

The Indian dancers rushed back to their seats, wrapping their gorgeous saris tightly around midriffs and plump breasts.

"That crude beast!" whispered angry parents. "That horrible deviate!" Their faces wore a uniform outrage.

The evening had again changed its direction. What had been intended as a harmless imitation of western contests had first become threatening, then suddenly soured. Mr. Patel admitted he did not know how to cope with the problem.

Victoria Fernandez was perhaps the only one prepared to meet the challenge. She did not return to her table. Instead, with flaring nostrils and arrogantly plucked eyebrows, she stood ready for any change in the rules of the contest. The greasy young men and women, her friends, formed a protective circle around her. The band, caught up in the beauty of its own music, remained totally calm in the face of such hatred. It sat like a tropical island, solid though buffeted, and played "I Feel Pretty" with touching recklessness.

"Man, I'm going to see this through," vowed Victoria Fernandez. "I'm thirty-six, twenty, thirty-eight, you know. Bring me a bathing costume, Mr. Patel. I don't scare so easily. Get me a costume and I'll be ready in two secs."

Victoria Fernandez was not destined to win that night. She was pretty and graceful, ambitious and sporting, and such qualities may generally be rewarded in beauty contests. But the evening had turned evil. It deepened the audience's capacity for shock and increased Antonia Whitehead's playfulness. Antonia began to tease Pronob, to whom earlier that morning she had given her paperback copy of the *Kama Sutra*. Ignoring the feelings of the people at her table, she described in detail what she called "the erotic vagaries" of Khajuraho and the Krishna legends. Pronob was by nature a nervous young man. The incidents of the early afternoon coupled with the evil of the evening totally undermined his strength.

"You aren't going to do anything foolish, are you?" he begged.

"Don't worry, Pronob." But Antonia's answer was not meant to comfort Pronob. She strode to the center of the hall, laughing and unzipping her dress as she went, then let it fall in a loop around her sandals till she was revealed to the world in her body stocking: an immense column of white flesh.

Next day the young men admitted that Antonia Whitehead had a commendable body. Their eyes were dull and glazed as they recalled the slipping of her floral chiffon dress. Then they reminded each other that the young woman had manly shoulders, tight little hips and negligible breasts, that her complexion was rude and savage, unsoothed by fresh cream or cucumber slices. But though they knew she was no *apsara* or Indian angel, they claimed that in their minds Darjeeling from that moment on somehow blended with the vision of an almost naked Miss Whitehead.

The competition for beauty queen lasted only a second. The white girl in body stocking galvanized noble emotions in the dining hall. Pride, humiliated sensitiveness, shock, fear locked the dim and dusky faces, demanding from Mr. Patel some last show of justice or revenge. Only the band, maliciously unresponsive to such feelings, continued to play "Lemon Tree" at its slow and tedious pace.

Mr. Patel was not equal to the responsibilities of the evening. He tried to behave naturally, cupping his hands, but allowing only rebellious ohs and ahs to escape. Then the Bengal Tiger jumped to his feet, his face like a sun in eclipse, lethal if viewed without a shade. He grabbed the damask cloth off his table, scattering crystal and champagne, *pilau*, *pakoras* and jeweled purses. He dragged the cloth with its spreading stains to the middle of the hall where Antonia Whitehead stood like a challenge, then he flung it over her pale and knotted shoulders. And each one in the room, dancers and diners alike, resident and nonresident guests, loved the Bengal Tiger for his quick reflexes and his infinite resourcefulness. They applauded him madly, shouting "Bravo!" and "Encore!" while some sensitive older women wept into handkerchiefs they had in happier days embroidered and tatted.

"What's happening to us?" cried the Bengal Tiger, having returned Antonia Whitehead to Pronob at the far end of his table. "I came here to rest. To breathe fresh air. What is this thing that has happened?" Then, pointing a stern finger at Mr. Patel, he instructed, "Manager-*babu*, please disqualify all contestants. Ladies and gentlemen, we better go to sleep. Otherwise all will be lost, our common sense and our happy-go-luckiness."

He gathered his party together, claimed his daughter from the judges' stand, where the Marwari sat sheepishly cleaning his fingernails with a toothpick, and he left.

"I must think of a new gimmick," said Mr. Patel to himself. He helped the waiters clear the dining room of guests and contestants. Then he waited for the rains so he could return to the plains, where he felt his life was infinitely more predictable and therefore safe.

5

THE BENGAL TIGER and his family returned to Calcutta the day before the rains were scheduled to start in Darjeeling.

"Hill diarrhea on top of everything else would be too much!"

The mountains had been magnificent, of course. But the holiday had been dismal. They had meant to see the sunrise from Tiger Hill, and drive down for a day to Kalimpong, but somehow the chance to do these things had never arisen. They came down to the plains unrefreshed by the fortnight in the hills.

In Calcutta the Bengal Tiger was quickly absorbed into his office routine. There were orders to track down and supply; junior executives to scold, dismiss and reinstate; import licenses to renew; and government officials to cajole. That left the Bengal Tiger little time to see to the emotional maladjustments of his family.

Tara and her mother worried that the Bengal Tiger would work himself sick. They tried to lure him away to Doris Day matinees on weekdays, but the Bengal Tiger appeared very displeased each time the women swooped into his office brandishing tickets for him. They schemed to save him from himself as they bought new saris or raised money for honest charities, but the Bengal Tiger remained bitterly uncooperative. Finally Arati planned a long weekend visit to Nayapur, a new township in a complex of coal mines, steel foundries and plants for hydro-electricity. At first the Bengal Tiger seemed enthusiastic about the weekend trip. He was anxious to show off Bengal's industrial progress to his daughter, and he instructed his secretary to reserve rooms for his party in the Nayapur Guest House. But two days before the Banerjees were scheduled to leave a business tangle developed and the Bengal Tiger had to fly to Delhi for a week. It was unthinkable for Tara's mother to leave her husband in the unloving hands of hotel servants, especially when his blood pressure was inordinately high after the holiday. She arranged for Aunt Jharna and her clubfooted little girl to move into Camac Street for a week.

Pronob's group feared that Tara would acquit herself badly with her aunt and suggested the whole group go off to Nayapur for an unusual weekend trip. Though their parents were unhappy (the mothers were convinced mixed picnics led to improperly romantic dreams), they entrusted Tara, the only married person, with the moral responsibilities of the picnic. When two maids were added to help Tara in her chaperoning duties, even Nilima was allowed by her mother to join the party.

Within days the whole city seemed to know of the projected trip to Nayapur. The Calcutta editor of the *Feminine Weekly* called the Bengal Tiger for permission to cover the weekend, and was told off roundly. Till the last minute before departure Pronob hoped Antonia Whitehead would accompany him. But Antonia had already left for a village in Bihar, saying, "Your friends put me off, Pronob. I've got work to do."

Nayapur can look gorgeous when viewed from the right angle. It spreads across scarred little hills and forests. The view is limitless and quite devastating. There are shiny roofs, long stretches of plate glass windows reflecting unbearable sunlight, chimneys, fires, smoke, trolleys, trucks.

Pronob's group arrived in Nilima's old Dodge station wagon very early on Friday morning. They followed erratic arrows that led to the Nayapur Guest House and reached a large bungalow hung with stiffly welcoming signs. The guest house seemed quite full; they had the feeling they had walked into a circus or a trap, and that the Calcutta editor of the *Feminine Weekly* was lying in wait for them inside the bungalow. They recognized Mr. Tuntunwala immediately. He was standing in the verandah surrounded by serious men in *dhoti*. When he noticed the newcomers, he forsook the serious men and thanked Sanjay for a recent editorial the young man had devoted to him. He shook hands with Tara, pointedly ignored Nilima and Reena, and invited everyone to his suite for lemonade.

The *chowkidar* and the *chowkidar*'s cousin, a recent arrival from his village, showed Pronob's group to their rooms. The girls were given one large room in the west wing, and the young men two rooms in the east wing. The *chowkidar*'s cousin, who spoke ambitious though scanty English, offered to bring the guests hot water for baths "and all special amenities."

Except for Tara, the group was reluctant to sample the industrial wonders of Nayapur. They ordered bucketfuls of hot water at seventy-five *naye paise* a bucket, breakfasted lightly on tea and eggs, then dedicated themselves to gin rummy. Tara, who disliked cards and had never mastered rummy or bridge, was rescued unexpectedly by Tuntunwala from her chaperoning duties.

"May I show you the township, Mrs. Cartwright?" he asked, pointing to a Land Rover parked in the shade of a mango tree. "It will honor me."

Tara, in spite of herself, was flattered by the attentions of a national hero. Tuntunwala had come to Nayapur to plan strategy for the final weeks of his election campaign. He left his ad-

visers arguing nastily over brochures in a corner of the verandah, and helped Tara into the Land Rover.

The countryside was overwhelming. Gigantic tracts had been
gouged out of green and romantic hills. Symmetrical layers had
been cut into the earth. Bulldozers, tractors, caterpillars, cement
mixers, the equipment of industrial progress, were reduced to
the size of roaches in that layered distance. After a while Tara
noted little clumps of buildings, neatly numbered and painted,
lit with neon, decorated with signboards that indicated the way
to reservoirs, foundries and dams. There were little residential
colonies also — small houses and gardens arranged in tidy files.
The colonies appeared sensible and dispassionate in the exaggerated violence of a landscape being fitted for industry and
progress.

Tuntunwala stopped the Land Rover on a rise and asked
Tara if the view before her compensated for the bumps and
lurches on the drive through unpaved trails. "It is truly a dignified place, don't you think, Mrs. Cartwright?"

Tara could come up with no appropriate words to his questions, and so said nothing.

"You don't like it?"

"Oh yes, I do. I'm just . . ."

"If there is an emotion to express one can always find a way of
expressing it, Mrs. Cartwright. Perhaps you don't have an emotion to express?"

"I love it, I love it. I'm terribly impressed."

"I want you to do one thing, please. I want you to shut your
eyes tightly and remember this scene in your head. This is my
favorite scene and I want to give you this memory as a present."

Tara was amused that a man like Tuntunwala was capable of
such imaginative games. She shut her eyes obediently and dismissed any suspicions she had initially entertained about him.

She did not know then that Tuntunwala had spoken very literally. Later he would commission an artist to paint him that landscape, and a bodyguard would deliver it to the Bengal Tiger's residence.

"You know, when I first started to come here this was a weritable jungle." He had told her she could open her eyes if she felt the scene had firmly impressed itself on her brain. "I could pick out small animals with my headlights. And once — no, I'm not joking — I shot a tiger near here, very decent-sized chap." Then because Tara looked unconvinced, he added, "If fate wills I can show you the selfsame tiger skin in my house one day?"

"I don't think fate will will any such thing."

"You're telling me I'm too bold a beggar, no? I'm sorry I offend you. I must curb my foolish impulses. Forget what I said about tiger skin, please."

Small talk was impossible between them. As long as they remained awed by the landscape they disposed of their fears of each other or their instinctive distrustfulness. But words required tact; words without tact left terrible consequences.

"What's that building there?" Tara asked, indicating a shiny roof at random.

Tuntunwala seized her question with gratitude and explained the function of that building, and of other buildings not indicated; he detailed the number, size and purpose of knobs, buttons, levers, charts and graphs that were inside those buildings. Tara quickly lost all interest, though she continued to supply him with well-timed questions. Tuntunwala was enchanted by his explanations. A procession of possibilities — what urbanization could mean for the rural electorate — must have passed through his head. He turned to her with increasing passion. "We can put electricity in every hut if the voters listen to me.

In fact, we can put a TV set in every hut if I'm elected."

"But think of the ads for bad breath, Mr. Tuntunwala."

"Call me by my good name please. Call me Pintoo because you are my friend."

"Think of the ads for deodorants and detergents."

Then he returned to making exclamations about the landscape. "It is such a fine and moving place! I experience redoubtable mental peace here. Looking at this scene I say to myself, India will be safe."

A prophetic light had overwhelmed the man. He leaned closer in the uncomfortable Land Rover and confided to Tara his dreams for industrial progress. Any remark that she could make she knew would be insufficient or inappropriate.

"We must make all our own machinery. We must do that before anything else."

"Don't you think you ought to worry about feeding the voters first?"

"You are for heart's matters, dear lady. You'd be no good in my Cabinet."

When they returned from the drive Tara discovered Pronob and his group had gone to an Uttam Kumar matinee in Nayapur's only movie theater.

"They have left you alone to cope with my wiles, Mrs. Cartwright?"

"Oh, no, they have left one of the maids. Besides, I'm the chaperon. *My* reputation is not at stake."

"And chaperons are irreproachable? Then there can be no scandal to my escorting you into the dining room while your friends are away?"

The waiter, who doubled as *chowkidar* to receive guests on their arrival at the bungalow, brought two handwritten menus, and stood beside their table with noticeable nervousness.

"Veg or non-veg?"

"Bring out both!" commanded Tuntunwala. "We're here on holiday, we mean to indulge ourselves."

The *chowkidar's* cousin flexed his muscles and saluted. "Very good, *sahib*. I bring *brinjal* curry, *dal* and *loochi* to begin with. But chicken curry excellent. I tried little bit in kitchen."

"Shut your mouth," whispered the sophisticated *chowkidar*. "My cousin-brother stupid villager. He did not try any food in the kitchen."

"Bring out the veg and the non-veg," repeated the National Personage.

The food when it appeared looked peppery and hot. Tara assumed it was delicious only because Tuntunwala devoured it at incredible speed. The long and bumpy ride in the Land Rover had given her a sick headache. Now the sight of the vegetarian and non-vegetarian meals being put away by a thin and temporarily amiable man accelerated her nausea. At first she was afraid to leave the table for fear of unnecessarily offending her lunch partner, but by the time the chicken had been ruthlessly chewed and its bones ground fine and discarded, she knew she would have to excuse herself and rush to the toilet.

"But you haven't touched your food yet!" Then he realized from the expression on Tara's face that perhaps more than food was involved in her illness. "You're not feeling well!"

Tuntunwala took charge at once. He led her out of the public dining room with authority while diners stared at him in anticipation of scandal or excitement. Tara was glad of his sympathy and even more of his offer of a homeopathic medicine that would cure her sick headache. He invited her to his suite to pick up the medicine. They were followed by the maid left behind in the guest house in case she was needed by Tara. The maid had fallen asleep before Tara returned from her drive, and she now blamed herself tearfully for whatever might have happened.

The Marwari's suite was the only air-conditioned one in the Nayapur Guest House. It also appeared to be better furnished than Tara's room. Tuntunwala settled Tara on a sofa that may have been meant for midgets, then went to the bathroom to mix the homeopathic drink. At Tara's feet the maid cursed herself extravagantly for having fallen asleep and permitted some undetermined calamity to overwhelm her mistress.

"Just stop making so much noise. The *missybaba* needs rest. Wait quietly in the verandah and I'll call you back when you are needed."

The man's tone was so authoritative, it did not occur to the maid to question the proprieties of his suggestion. Tara knew she should protest. Yet she couldn't. It would be useless to storm out now. She was tired, and sick; she was curious and impatient. She could wait a few minutes longer. If she were a more aggressive young woman, better able to protect herself like Antonia Whitehead, she knew she would have walked out of the suite with the maid. But she was neither forceful nor impulsive. At that moment the Marwari appeared to her strong, sensible and curiously akin to the Bengal Tiger and Hari Lal Banerjee.

While Tuntunwala held a glass of fetid yellow liquid in front of her Tara thought she loved David desperately. How absurd that she had feared she was incapable of affection! How pathetic that she had worried about sinking into Calcutta's vast sadness! She saw a procession of children eating yoghurt off Park Street, rude men chasing horses in Darjeeling, a marcher subdued near the Catelli, and she whispered, "It isn't possible in Bengal. We're sensitive, we're sentimental, it can't happen to Bengalis."

But Tuntunwala had decided to ignore her tender feelings. "Please try to relax. Please continue to sit tight. I'll rub some

Vicks VapoRub on your forehead. I've found it excellent for all headaches and nervous crises."

Tara gathered herself primly on the small sofa. "No thanks," she said. But Tuntunwala was accustomed only to acquiescence, to disposing of business empires and petty destinies without advice or apology. He dismissed her "No thanks" with a sympathetic nod, and began rubbing Vicks VapoRub indulgently on her forehead. Tara resorted to small talk; it had ruined an entente between them earlier in the day and she thought she could count on her tactlessness to do so again. "What are you *really* doing here this weekend, Mr. Tuntunwala?"

"Planning strategy."

"You expect to win?"

"In heart's matters, yes."

She was hurt by his confidence. She turned away from him and worried that the lunch of uneaten chicken, the headache, the homeopathic drink and the Vicks VapoRub had led only to this pitiful attempt at promiscuity. Then Tuntunwala changed to a gentler tone.

"Please, please," he said, clutching Tara with sticky fingers. "I'm given to unfortunate impulses. You can't surely break from me now?"

"Really!"

"There is no time for coy preliminaries. You're liberated and advanced and I admire you greatly."

"Admiration is no reason for yielding to what you suggest!"

"I do not think you will leave, Mrs. Cartwright — how will you explain it to your maid?"

The Marwari sat on the arm of Tara's sofa, looking most unhappy. Then slowly the disappointment paled and was succeeded by dull anger. "I think you have no choice," he said, putting away the jar of Vicks.

In another Calcutta such a scene would not have happened. Tara would not have walked into the suite of a gentleman for medicine, and a gentleman would not have dared to make such improper suggestions to her. But except for Camac Street, Calcutta had changed greatly; and even Camac Street had felt the first stirrings of death. With new dreams like Nayapur Tara's Calcutta was disappearing. New dramas occurred with each new bulldozer incision in the green and romantic hills. Slow learners like Tara were merely victims.

6

THE SEDUCTION of Tara had been tastefully executed by Tuntunwala, and the maid in the corridor remained ignorant of all untoward details. There were no apologies or recriminations. Tuntunwala assumed that "heart's matters" were unimportant. He invited her to join him for tea, then went to the next room to confer with the serious men in *dhoti* who were planning his campaign. Tara's first reaction had been to complain to Sanjay and Pronob, to tell them Tuntunwala was a parasite who would survive only at their expense. But the outrage soon subsided, leaving a residue of unforgiving bitterness. She realized she could not share her knowledge of Tuntunwala with any of her friends. In a land where a friendly smile, an accidental brush of the fingers, can ignite rumors — even lawsuits — how is one to speak of Mr. Tuntunwala's violence? The others would have to make their own compromises. Tara wrote them a note saying that she had suddenly taken ill. Then, accompanied by the useless maid, she left immediately for Camac Street by train.

In Camac Street her parents found her bitterness inexplicable. She talked constantly of returning to David, and in their efforts to encourage her to remain longer with them they suggested intellectual pastimes like poetry readings and visits to the nuns at St. Blaise's. Their love for her was so great that they arranged a coffee-house poet to read in their own house. The deliberately dirty and vituperous young man recited his anatomical verses on the lawn, then demanded some cutlets and sweetmeats for the other "Hungry Generation" poets in his mess.

The nuns at St. Blaise's were more sympathetic than the avant-garde poet. They seemed to Tara browner than she remembered, their accents more Indian than she had expected. They fluttered around her in the parlor, anxious for news and for snaps of her husband. They were hysterical with pleasure when she produced a passport-size photograph of an amused young man in glasses; then she read them a paragraph from David's latest letter because she considered his observation frighteningly appropriate.

I have been reading a biography of William James, with all of *his* innumerable trips through the Continent. The trips you describe in India seem so nineteenth centuryish, so beware of highwaymen, my dear . . .

Mother Peter Ignatius was distraught with pleasure at the revelation of photograph and confidential letter; she begged permission to include the paragraph in the alumna column of the school magazine she edited. Then the nuns showed her embroidered sandwich covers, lace doilies, tablecloths and pillowcases that the "poor girls" had made in a branch of their convent to assure her that nothing had changed at St. Blaise's. Tara was moved to buy a dozen doilies, then with bitter regret she left the nuns standing on the school steps. All her early ideas of love, fair play and good manners had come from those women. Now as she saw them in their quaint formation on the steps of St. Blaise's, they seemed to her people in a snapshot, yellow and faded.

David's letters during the monsoons also intensified her depression. He wrote that he had been reading Ved Mehta's journals on India, and that even in New York they brought home to him the dangers that surrounded her every day. He told Tara he saw Calcutta as the collective future in which garbage, disease, and stagnation are man's estate. "Survival to the lower forms, insects and sludgeworms." Though the Bengal Tiger tried to protect her from the excesses of the city, Tara told her parents that she was preparing to return to David and the United States.

On the first rainless day in August Tara went to the Air India office and reserved a seat for herself on a flight to New York leaving at the end of the week. Then, because she was given to serious and sentimental farewells, she telephoned Reena, Pronob and Sanjay to meet her at the Catelli-Continental that afternoon so she could break the news to them.

The Bengal Tiger and his wife were helpless in the face of Tara's new and implacable determination. They brightened up a little when Sanjay came in his Fiat to drive their daughter to the Catelli-Continental. They hoped the group would succeed in delaying Tara's departure. It was seven years since they had last seen her, and they convinced themselves that they would never see her again. They watched the PRESS sticker on Sanjay's car disappear from their compound, and because they were affectionate and clannish they hoped life would be kinder to Tara than it had been to them. They called for an early tea and prayed that the riots would not interrupt the last days of Tara's holiday.

In the car Tara was careful not to respond with cynicism to

Sanjay's praise of Tuntunwala as a candidate. She felt she had made her peace with the city, nothing more was demanded. If she were to stay, she thought, there would be other concessions, other deals and compromises, all menacing and unbearably real, waiting to be made.

The crowds on the way to the hotel seemed more than usually impertinent. At traffic lights and intersections they threatened to overturn the car and burn its occupants. The refugees on the sidewalk were gathering together their pots and pans and children, rolling up sleeping mats and putting away coins. They seemed to be taking precautions against some foreseeable damage.

Under a striped umbrella of the Catelli-Continental Pronob told the group he had heard rumors that a procession was on its way to the *maidan*, that it would go right by the hotel and rally near the monument. The waiters completed the details. A boy had been run over by a tram and killed; he had been carrying a heavy can of oil for his mother when his foot slipped on the tracks. An angry crowd had tried to lynch the tram conductor, and when the police had frustrated them by arresting the man, the crowd had lain in wait for the next tram, dragged its conductor out and beaten him to death. Now the crowd, still unappeased and swelling, were marching over to the *maidan*'s monument.

Tara realized the moment was inappropriate for the breaking of sentimental news. A mob was approaching Chowringhee from the south. The young men in front were armed with bamboo poles and axes. Some of them wore handkerchiefs knotted over their heads. At times they lifted the kerchiefs to wipe sweat off their foreheads and necks. Some carried whistles, which they blew shrilly to punctuate slogans. Their gestures were those of rebellious children rather than political militants. Many joked and laughed and ate peanuts from paper cones. Tara's friends were furious; they told each other it had been a bad idea to meet at the Catelli on such a day.

A contingent of policemen soon appeared. They looked very spruce, still in starched turbans and short pants, twirling their *lathi* and fingering their belts. A group of young and beardless marchers darted out of the procession and punched two policemen. But they were driven back far into the mob, bleeding from cuts on their faces or heads. The marshals of the procession shouted orders to each other, argued vociferously, then scolded the groups nearest them. A young woman in braids threw down her cardboard sign and sat on the curb to rest. There were children among the marchers, and they were holding new toys, perhaps liberated from shops on the way. A toothless old man walking his dog beside the marchers was persuaded to carry an extra pennant.

The excitement of the riot overwhelmed Reena. She stood by the parapet, exclaiming at the mob and encouraging the policemen. Then she waved in the direction of a very handsome young man in uniform, leaning against the side of a police jeep.

Reena pointed to his revolver and the little swagger stick he carried and addressed him as "old Popo," because he had roomed with her cousin at college. He was too far away, of course, to hear her. But she cupped her hands and leaned over the parapet. "Right on!" she shouted. "Power to old Popo! Right on, I say!"

The discovery of "old Popo" in the mob reassured Pronob's group that fair play would still prevail in Calcutta that day. At first the anonymity of the rioters had frightened them. But now that they had recognized a face in that confusion of marchers and policemen they felt reasonably sure they could predict how the day would end. They called the waiter to their table to order more coffee, then settled down to enjoying the spectacle below them.

"You know, I'm beginning to think I was wrong about that Tuntunwala chap," confessed Pronob as he waited for the Catelli waiter to bring him an espresso. "If he's elected, things like this won't happen again."

Tara agreed with him, but with pointed nastiness, and was rebuked by Sanjay. In recent weeks the editor had relied solely on fierce passion to convince his readers that Tuntunwala was a prophet.

"This is no time for petty suspicions, Tara. This is crisis time for all of us, so be sensible if nothing else."

A frail woman in the street hurled a soda bottle against a confectioner's window on Chowringhee Avenue. Soon dirty men and children were running in and out of the store, carrying fancy cakes shaped like hearts or diamonds, some with marzipan clowns or brides on them. They tossed cookies to each other, let them fall into the street, then darted between legs to collect them in handkerchiefs and save them for hungrier moments. A very dark man in striped boxer shorts carried a radio on his head and danced in and out of his line in the procession. Suddenly there was a loud explosion, and the man fell flat on his back, and someone else picked up the radio and disappeared into an alley. Quickly and violently all cars were being stopped by either the marchers or the police. Passengers were ordered to run to safety, so they abandoned their cars in the middle of the street. In the distance a car was still smoking and handcuffed boys were being pushed into police trucks. A motorcyclist, moving slowly and noisily down the length of the procession, was shoved by a marcher from behind; he fell on the street and his motorcycle careened into the mob without him. There were screams and curses. People surged out of the way of the motorcycle. A young man lifted a boy who had been knocked unconscious by the machine. Slogans were shrill and triumphant around the young man holding the boy. The marshals waved the crowd on. The *maidan* was slowly filling.

Tara was not immune to such casual madness. She plunged into terrified chatter about airplane tickets and reservations and David and Katherine Mansfield. An agitated waiter in a torn turban pleaded with the patrons of the Catelli to go home before the hotel was sacked. Diners overturned delicate rattan chairs in their anxiety to be first in the elevator. Apprehensive managers walked from table to table, asking, "Was the service satisfactory, sir? No need to panic. This hotel is burglar-proof and safer than the streets." A little girl cried into her ice-cream cone as she ran with her mother to the fire exit. Young women in pale georgette saris stood on glass-topped tables weeping inconsolably. A businessman in a three-piece suit took off his socks and shoes to make his getaway easy. An old man in a blazer sitting beside a potted palm counted change from his pocket for the waiter's tip.

The threat of riot seemed to bring out the best in Pronob. He was suddenly full of passionate sententiousness. He talked of "Calcutta's final curtain," of "mad dogs and beasts" and "heroic survivors" as he organized his group for a dash down the staircase and into Sanjay's car parked across the street. Fat women wearing diamonds dug their elbows under Tara's chin. A pudgy boy in sailor outfit was pushed against the railing and started to cry when the balloon he had been holding burst at the end of its long string. "Bang on!" Reena kept whispering as she carved a path for herself and her friends among the thick and frightened bodies. Halfway down the carpeted staircase Tara's jeweled aqua sandals came apart and she tripped. Pronob pulled her up and dragged her down the rest of the way. He flung the torn sandal on the receptionist's counter as the crowd pushed him toward the Catelli's doorway. There were posters of Tuntunwala on the counter top, brochures and flags announcing his candidacy. A beardless young man resembling Tuntunwala but without the older man's hardness or authority stood behind the counter, waving to the Catelli patrons to behave sensibly.

When Pronob escorted his group to the door of the hotel, a splinter mob tried to force him back into the foyer. They were fierce men and women. They smashed glass panels with bricks they had brought with them. They struck the doorkeeper again and again; just before he fell the doorkeeper shouted to Pronob to hurry back inside the hotel.

"Press! Press!" shouted Sanjay. The crowd parted slightly, absorbed the four friends, then disgorged them on the other side of the street. They ran to Sanjay's Fiat as the mob pressed against the sides of the car, pointed to soda bottles and bamboo sticks, and shook tiny fists at the four people inside. Then a bomb exploded somewhere. A storefront collapsed. Looters carried off sheets and towels. Sullen policemen arrived swinging *lathi*. Marchers kicked Sanjay's Fiat as they ran toward the steps of the hotel. There was no way Sanjay could back his car out into the street. The friends crouched in the little car with doors locked and windows rolled tight. Now and then a stone or broken bottle hurled against a door and chipped paint off the Fiat. The empty taxi on their left was dented badly, its tires slashed and headlights missing. Young boys were working on it methodically, carrying out detachable ashtrays and light bulbs, and destroying what they could not carry. On the other side of the street a bus was burning slowly. People spat on the windows of Sanjay's car, rattled the locked door handles and made obscene gestures at the girls crying inside.

A confrontation was shaping up outside the Catelli-Continental. The doorkeeper lay on his side under the striped awning and a beggar girl with tangled hair sat on his high stool instead. Tuntunwala suddenly came out of the hotel. He stood on the steps, stubborn and dispassionate. "Old Popo" was conferring seriously with him. Rows of constables were called and lined up near the doorway. They held their *lathi* horizontally and the mob withdrew a few feet. A middle-aged man in an undershirt and loose pajamas threw a stone through the open door and was wrestled to the ground before he had barely finished throwing.

Tara watched Tuntunwala guarding the entrance of the Catelli-Continental and thought of something even lower than a parasite, something that had evolved beyond the need for higher forms. In that moment of terror, in a closed car before a mob, she felt she was being used by some force that was too large for her to manage.

"Have you seen *Pather Panchali?*" she asked.

"What a stupid question! Who hasn't?"

"Do you remember all that greenery? Do you remember Apu running through those forests?" Tara asked.

"I remember the greenery in black and white."

"What's happened to those forests, Pronob? What killed them?"

"Really, Tara! How dare you talk such nonsense at a time like this!"

"Old Popo" was shouting into a megaphone. "Please fall back, everyone. Please fall back. This hotel is the private property of Mr. Tuntunwala."

The crowd surged backward and forward, then retreated toward the line of cars parked across the street.

"Please fall back or we will be forced to adopt drastic measures. This is a warning."

Two marchers jumped on the hood of Sanjay's Fiat as the crowd pushed back farther and farther. From the *maidan* someone hurled a brick and it crashed through the windshield of the dented taxi.

Then an old man in a blazer rushed out of the Catelli-Continental. He was stopped by Tuntunwala and a constable, but the old man shook himself free and snatched the megaphone from Popo's hand.

"Mrs. Cartwright!" he shouted. "Are you there, dear lady? Are you still there somewhere?"

"What's wrong with him?"

"*Here I am* . . . Mrs. Cartwright . . . *an old man* . . . The year of the puppy is over, do you understand? The age of snakes is coming but the boy doesn't know it yet."

"He's absolutely daft!"

"*We who seven years ago spoke of honor,* Madam . . ."

"Here, you, give that thing back to me!"

"Crows are picking at corpses, Mrs. Cartwright. The fires we saw are frozen."

"Tara, that's your weird friend out there!"

"You can't allow him to continue like this, Inspector! He's a weritable nuisance!"

"Can you hear me? Can you hear? Already half of Calcutta, surely half of . . . *bats with baby faces.*"

"Will you do it or shall I call my bodyguards?"

"*I have no ghosts,* Mrs. Cartwright."

"Sir, it's my job, and I'll have you know I take all my jobs very seriously."

"Kisses were tattooed on our foreheads. Rust on walls can kill, did you guess that?"

"Oh, for heaven's sake, Tara, your friend's going to make Tuntunwala look like a fool!" exclaimed Sanjay.

"Why doesn't he get out of the way?"

"They'll hurt him! They've no choice!"

"*After such knowledge* . . . tail devoured by head as always
. . . and then . . ."

"He's crazy. You want me to hit a crazy man, sir?"

"He's not a madman at all. I weritably believe he's been sent
by the other side."

"Dear Madam, you *I shored against my ruins.* Have you left?
Where are the jets?"

"Okay, you had your chance. Now I'll call my own guards."

There was a scuffle on the steps of the Catelli-Continental.
Amplified and distorted groans came through the megaphone,
which was now lying on the sidewalk under the striped awning.
Four men in livery had wrestled the old man to the ground.
His ascot had come undone, and his gray hair was dusty. The
men in livery played with him a bit, then threw him lightly like
a handball into the mob, and the mob fell on him immediately.

They were not kind to Joyonto Roy Chowdhury, those
marchers in undershirts and ragged *dhoti.* They kicked him
and scratched him and tossed him from line to line. A bruise
spread across his face, and there was a cut under his chin. They
tore off his blazer, and flung the brass buttons at his cheek. Giggling youths tried the blazer on for size, made funny faces to
each other, then ripped it viciously with pocketknives.

"My God! They're not content to kill him!"

"Your friend's a bloody fool, Tara! But I can't let them do
this to him!"

"Pronob! Don't, please! There's nothing you can do."

"How dare they do that to an old man like him!"

"Pronob! What is this nonsense, please? They'll get you
too!"

But Pronob was out of the car before anyone could stop him.

He got only two steps away when the mob seized him. A soda bottle burst against Pronob's head. He had no time to scream. Tara had not seen so much blood on a friend before; a fat man bleeds profusely. They punched him while he was still bleeding. Pronob fell against the side of the taxi and they kept punching. He would never know that his gesture had been useless, that "Old Popo" had rescued Joyonto before the crowd could kill him.

Above Chowringhee Avenue the vision that had teased Tara all summer, the vision that had made Joyonto sometimes feel almost holy, bounced off banners and picket signs, boxed the ears of a looting urchin and pinched the bottom of a female revolutionary, and spread hysteria in the city.

And Tara, still locked in a car across the street from the Catelli-Continental, wondered whether she would ever get out of Calcutta, and if she didn't, whether David would ever know that she loved him fiercely.